DOCTOR WHO
INFERNO

Based on the BBC television serial by Don Houghton by
arrangement with the British Broadcasting Corporation

TERRANCE DICKS

Number 89
in the
Doctor Who Library

TARGET

A TARGET BOOK

published by
the Paperback Division of
W. H. ALLEN & Co. PLC

A Target Book
Published in 1984
By the paperback Division of
W.H. Allen & Co. PLC
44 Hill Street, London W1X 8LB

First published in Great Britain by
W.H. Allen & Co. PLC 1984

Printed and bound in Great Britain by
Hunt Barnard Printing Ltd, Aylesbury, Bucks.

ISBN 0 426 19617 1

CONTENTS

1	Project Inferno	7
2	The Beast	15
3	Mutant	25
4	The Slime	31
5	Dimension of Terror	40
6	The Nightmare	48
7	Death Sentence	58
8	Countdown to Doom	66
9	Penetration-Zero	75
10	The Monsters	84
11	Escape Plan	89
12	Doomsday	96
13	Return to Danger	104
14	The Last Mutation	112
15	The Doctor Takes a Trip	120

1

Project Inferno

It was the greatest scientific project that England had ever known. More technologically advanced than nuclear power. Potentially, far more lucrative than North Sea Oil. The Stahlman project. Or as those who worked on it called it – the Inferno.

An audacious scheme to drill through to the untapped energy-sources at the Earth's core. Unimaginable, unending heat. A fuel gas that would power every home, every shop, every factory in Britain. Limitless free energy for everyone.

That was the promise, and the Government, hypnotised by the force and conviction of Professor Stahlman's arguments, dazzled by the prospect of economic problems solved forever, poured money and resources into the project. There was a sort of unspoken agreement – the Stahlman project had to succeed.

Now the project was nearing completion.

Hungry for the long-awaited success, the authorities were deaf to the steadily increasing warnings about the project's dangers – dangers that might, just conceivably, involve the end of the world.

Some of these warnings came from the unpaid, unofficial Scientific Adviser to the organisation responsible for project security, an organisation called UNIT – the United Nations Intelligence Taskforce.

He was an odd-looking fellow, this Scientific Adviser, tall and thin and beaky-nosed with an old/young face and a mane of prematurely white hair. He dressed oddly too, in ruffled shirt and elegant velvet smoking-jacket, the ensemble completed by a long, flowing cape.

The strangest thing of all was that he didn't seem to have a name. He was known only as the Doctor . . .

Singing '*La donna é mobile*' in a loud, cheerful and rather tuneless voice, the Doctor drove Bessie, his converted, souped-up Edwardian roadster, through the sprawling complex of low buildings surrounded by storage towers, gantries, access roads and railway-lines that made up the Stahlman project.

It was a messy, unattractive-looking area, the site of a now-disused oil refinery. Some of the buildings and facilities had been taken over by Stahlman and his team, others left derelict. Dominating everything were two brand new structures. One was the massive, metallically gleaming drill tower, housing the drill which was now boring its way relentlessly to the centre of the earth. Its steady roar could be heard all over the project area. Not far away was the low concrete bunker containing the nuclear reactor. The drilling needed colossal amounts of power.

Considering the fact that he regarded the entire project as a ridiculous and very dangerous waste of money, and that he had a positive distaste for Professor Stahlman, its Director, the Doctor was in a remarkably jovial mood. These were still the early days of his exile to the planet Earth by the Time Lords. He still had hopes of evading their sentence and getting his somewhat erratic space/time craft, the TARDIS, operational again. For that, he would need power – and the Stahlman project had power to burn.

'La donna é mobile,' carolled the Doctor cheerfully. 'Dee-dah-dah dum-dah-dah!' Waving to a passing technician, the Doctor drove on.

The technician was a drill-head rigger called Harry Slocum. Returning the Doctor's wave, he got off his bike, parked it and lugged his tool-box over to the main control centre.

In the doorway he ran into one of his mates, a technician called Bromley.

Slocum raised his voice above the sound of the drill. 'Hullo, John, how's it going in there?'

Bromley shrugged. 'Still drilling away!'

'You make it sound like the dentists!' said Slocum

cheerfully. He made his way in to main control and stood looking around him.

The huge control-room had its usual air of remorseless, almost robotic efficiency. White-coated technicians moved purposefully amongst the instrument banks that lined the walls, constantly checking readings and adjusting power-levels. The far end of the room was dominated by the giant computer, which, in theory, guided and monitored every stage of the drilling operation. Close by was the countdown indicator, a digital clock indicating the time left before estimated penetration. As Slocum entered the room, the indicator read 72:18:35. Seventy two hours, eighteen minutes and thirty-five seconds.

Gazing worriedly up at the indicator was a plumpish bespectacled man in a business suit and a mildly incongruous bow-tie. This was Sir Keith Gold, Executive Director of the project.

Slocum made his way over to him. 'Excuse me, Sir Keith? You asked for someone from Maintenance?'

'Yes, indeed. Thank you for coming so promptly. I want you to have a look at number 2 output, if you would be so good.'

Slocum smiled, tickled as always by Sir Keith's old-fashioned politeness. 'On the blink is she?'

'I've had it taken out of service – we've switched over to 1 and 3.'

'Right you are. Let's take a look.'

Sir Keith led the way to the tunnel that connected main control to the separate drill-head section. This was a smaller area, starkly metallic and functional, with a control console set into one wall. In the centre, surrounded by a low metal rampart, was a colossal semi-transparent tube that ran from floor to ceiling. It was surrounded by a complex of power cables and metal pipes that ran from the base of the central column and disappeared into the floor. The output pipes sucked up and cleared away the debris thrown up by the robot drill-head, now almost twenty miles beneath their feet.

Slocum went over to number 2 output and knelt to examine it. The massive metal pipe was made up of jointed sections and one of the sections had buckled slightly, causing a tiny gap to appear.

Slocum straightened up. 'Okay, I'll fix it.'

'As quickly as possible, if you please. Professor Stahlman doesn't want any delay.'

'Don't worry about it, Sir Keith. Doesn't look too serious.'

Sir Keith nodded his thanks and turned away – then froze as he saw a burly figure glowering at him from the entrance of the tunnel. Professor Stahlman wore a crisp white lab coat over a dark suit not unlike Sir Keith's own. Somehow, with Stahlman the effect was stiffly formal, almost military. Yet at the same time there was something almost primitive about the man's bulky broad-shouldered body and massive close-cropped head, the neatly trimmed beard thrust aggressively forwards. He looked like a gorilla in a lab coat, reflected Sir Keith, immediately ashamed of the uncharitable thought. He braced himself for the coming encounter. Somehow a meeting with Stahlman always was an encounter – a confrontation.

Stahlman's voice was unexpectedly mild. 'Ah, Sir Keith. Why has the drilling rate been slowed down?'

'Number 2 output pipe is out of service,' said Sir Keith defensively. 'Naturally we had to decelerate, since . . .'

'I do understand the technical problems, Sir Keith,' interrupted Stahlman silkily.

'Naturally, I didn't mean to imply otherwise . . .'

'What I do not understand is why you took it upon yourself to interfere.' Stahlman's voice suddenly lashed out, like a whip.

Sir Keith flushed. 'I saw the report of the malfunction some time ago. When I saw no report of its repair, I assumed that you had overlooked . . .'

'I overlook nothing, Sir Keith. The malfunction is not sufficiently serious to warrant a deceleration of the drilling rate – *and you have no authority to order one.*'

'As Executive Director of this project – '

'As Executive Director of the project, Sir Keith, your concern is with such vital matters as the facilities of the canteen and the new duty-roster for the cleaners. Anything to do with drilling is my concern, and mine alone. And that includes minor maintenance problems.'

10

'Surely, in a project such as this there can be no such thing as a minor problem?'

Professor Stahlman sighed. 'I'll make a bargain with you, Sir Keith. You stay away from my drilling operation – and I'll let you run your canteen!' Stahlman turned away dismissively.

After a moment, the now thoroughly routed Sir Keith hurried out of the drill area.

Doing his best to ignore this embarrassing scene between his superiors, Harry Slocum finished replacing and re-bolting the warped pipe section. He noticed a smear of some dark-green substance at the point where the old section joined the new. Curiously he touched it – and snatched his hand away. A terrible burning sensation swept through his entire body.

He examined his fingers in horror, expecting to find them badly burned. But there was only a tiny, dark-green stain . . . Wiping his fingers on his overalls, Slocum began packing away his tools. Suddenly he felt very strange. He was almost unbearably hot, and nothing seemed quite real.

Flu, thought Slocum, or some kind of fever. He had better report sick.

Back in the main control area, Sir Keith was talking to an attractive white-coated young woman, with a pleasant open face framed by long fair hair. Her name was Petra Williams. She was Professor Stahlman's personal assistant.

'But why is he so unreasonable?' asked Sir Keith plaintively. 'You would think I was some kind of rival, an enemy even.'

Petra did her best to defend her 'chief's' behaviour. 'He's worked on this one project for many years. Naturally he feels possessive about it.'

Sir Keith nodded, trying to make allowances. Eric Stahlman had grown up in the ruins of post-war Germany. To have reached his present eminence must have taken years of terrible struggle against unimaginable difficulties. Stahlman was brilliant, no doubt of that. They would just have to bear with him.

But mild as he was, Sir Keith had a streak of obstinacy.

He had no intention of allowing Stahlman to endanger the safety of others.

'I've got another piece of news he won't care for, Petra. Maybe you'd better break it to him.'

'Oh? What's that?'

'I've sent for a drilling consultant, a chap called Greg Sutton. One of the most experienced oilmen in the world.'

'But this isn't an oil rig. The whole operation is run on completely different lines.'

'Nevertheless, I should feel happier if *someone* on this project knew a little more about the purely practical aspects of drilling – and its dangers.'

Petra sighed. 'So when does this expert arrive?'

'Any minute now. He's flying in from Kuwait.'

Engrossed in their conversation, neither Petra nor Sir Keith noticed that Harry Slocum, tool-kit abandoned, was walking slowly out of the tunnel, a strange, dazed expression on his face. He had a ghastly greenish pallor, and he clutched a massive pipe-wrench in his right hand.

Professor Stahlman had seen him go, but he had scarcely registered Slocum's appearance. To Stahlman the technician's departure meant only that the repair job was finished.

He turned to a nearby technician. 'Put number 2 pipe back into service. Accelerate drilling speed three and a half per cent. We now have to make up for lost time!'

Harry Slocum staggered out of the building and stumbled aimlessly across a stretch of open ground. He stopped, hands over his ears. A low, sinister screeching sound was sounding inside his head.

A technician turned the corner of the building, stopped in astonishment, and then hurried towards him, assuming that Slocum must be ill. He came up behind him and put a hand on his shoulder. 'Harry? What's the matter?'

Slocum swung around, and the other man stepped back in horror. Slocum's face was that of a wild beast, eyes glowing red, lips drawn back in a savage snarl.

The technician had only seconds to register the terrifying sight. Then Slocum's pipe-wrench came crashing down on his head.

The Brigadier's new office might only be a converted storeroom off main control, but it was the Brigadier's office for all that, and Sergeant Benton was determined that it should do UNIT credit. The place was spotlessly clean. The Brigadier's files and papers were arranged in impeccable order, and the newly installed telephone was working perfectly.

Benton was proudly arranging the finishing touch – one of the Brigadier's collection of regimental photographs – when the door swung open and the Brigadier himself marched into the room.

Sergeant Benton put the photograph carefully down on the desk and crashed to attention. 'Sir!'

The Brigadier touched the peak of his cap with his cane, returning the salute. 'Morning, Benton.' He gazed around the room.

'Best they could do for us on such short notice,' said Sergeant Benton apologetically.

The Brigadier nodded. 'It'll do. Have you contacted the Doctor?'

'On his way over, sir.'

'Anything on this chap Slocum yet?'

'Lads are still looking, sir.'

'Still?'

'It's a big rambling place this, sir, and Slocum knows it a lot better than we do. If we sent for more men, or sent out a general alarm . . . '

'No, not yet. We don't want a panic.'

The Doctor strolled casually into the room. 'Hullo, Brigadier, making yourself at home?'

'How are you, Doctor?'

'Just getting myself settled in – ' The Doctor broke off picking up the photograph from the desk. 'Good heavens! Which one's you Brigadier? No, let me guess.' He studied the rows of faces, then looked up defeated. 'None of them?'

'Fifth from the left, third row,' said the Brigadier impassively.

The Doctor looked again at the photograph and shook his head. 'I don't believe it. I can see why you grew that moustache!'

Sergeant Benton's lips twitched – until a swift glance from the Brigadier reduced him to frozen-faced immobility.

The Brigadier said, 'Trouble seems to follow you, doesn't it, Doctor?'

'What *do* you mean?'

'You persuade me to allow you and Miss Shaw to join me on this project as observers – '

'Allow?' said the Doctor indignantly. 'Allow? Miss Shaw may have the misfortune to work for you, Brigadier, but I am a free agent.'

The Brigadier ignored this. 'And then, within a few days of your arrival, I have a motiveless murder on my hands.' The Brigadier looked at Benton. 'Wrench?'

'Here, sir.' Benton took a tray from one of the shelves and handed it to the Brigadier, who placed it on the desk in front of the Doctor. 'Yesterday afternoon one of the maintenance technicians was beaten to death – with this.'

The Doctor studied the wrench. 'Do you know who did the killing?'

'This wrench was found next to the body. It belongs to a drill-head rigger called Harry Slocum. We're still looking for him.'

'Do you know anything about him?'

The Brigadier looked at Benton, who said, 'Seems to have been one of the most popular men on the complex, sir.'

'There's something else,' said the Brigadier slowly. 'Try touching it, Doctor.'

The Doctor touched the wrench cautiously with one finger. 'It's warm.'

'When it was first found it was hot – red-hot, almost as though it had been in a furnace.' The Brigadier sat back. 'Well, Doctor? Any theories?'

2

The Beast

The Doctor stood very still for a moment, peering thoughtfully down at the wrench. 'If it had absorbed an immense amount of energy . . .' he muttered. 'Perhaps that could have disturbed the atomic make-up in some way . . .' His voice trailed off.

The Brigadier turned to Benton. 'Chase up those patrols, Sergeant. I want this man Slocum found.'

'Sir!' Benton saluted and marched away.

The Brigadier turned back to the Doctor, who seemed lost in thought. 'Doctor, why were you so keen to observe this project?'

The Doctor gave him a rather startled look. 'Well, er, it's an event of great scientific interest, my dear feller. The first penetration of the Earth's crust! Naturally I'm interested.'

'Yes, of course,' said the Brigadier.

'Well, I must be off,' said the Doctor hurriedly. 'I should concentrate on finding that missing rigger if I were you. You'll have to excuse me now, Brigadier, Miss Shaw and I have work to do.'

'You're actually taking part in the project?'

'Well, in a sense . . . Some – related experiments. Goodbye for now, Brigadier.'

Greg Sutton had complained bitterly in Kuwait, he had protested on the plane, and he was still grumbling as Sir Keith Gold marched him into the drill-head area.

'So, I get snatched off the rig in Kuwait just when I'm sure we've made a strike, flown back so fast me stomach's still over the Med, and I still haven't got the slightest idea what I'm supposed to be doing here!'

15

Sutton was a burly, broad-shouldered man in a linen suit, with a pleasantly ugly face and a sun-baked, wind-weathered complexion.

Sir Keith said, 'I'm afraid it's all my fault, Mr Sutton. I asked the Government for a top oil-rig man, and you're the man they sent me.'

'Very flattering. This is a Government project, right? So now I'm some kind of Civil Servant?'

'Well, broadly speaking. How do you like the idea?'

'No comment,' said Sutton dryly. He was surveying the drill-head area in some astonishment. 'And what's this contraption supposed to be?'

'This, Mr Sutton is the drill-head.'

'You're joking.'

'It *is* a drill-head, Mr Sutton, I assure you. The only one of its kind in the world.'

'How deep?'

'Twenty miles.'

'Twenty miles? You'd get such a whip in the drill-pipes they'd fracture.'

'No pipes, Mr Sutton. A robot drill with its own built-in power source. Fed by those cables with power from our own nuclear reactor.'

Sutton shook his head wonderingly. 'Twenty miles. You're liable to wake up old Nick himself going that deep.'

Sir Keith said wryly, 'Some of our technicians have nicknamed this operation Project Inferno.'

'So what's it all in aid of?'

'Soon we shall be able to penetrate the Earth's crust and tap the pockets of Stahlman's Gas which lie beneath it.'

'What do you do with it when you've got it?'

'According to Professor Stahlman, the originator of the project, it will be, quote, "a vast new storehouse of energy which has lain dormant since the beginning of time", unquote.'

'Well, you learn something new every day.' Sutton studied the tangle of different-sized pipes and cables around the drill-head with a professional eye. 'What do these big pipes here do? And these smaller ones?'

'The big output pipes carry the debris away from the drill-

16

head. These others carry a coolant chemical down to the bore. You see the basic principle . . .'

Greg Sutton listened patiently as Sir Keith explained the purpose and the working methods of the project in greater detail. Finally, he said, 'Okay, Sir Keith, I get the picture. But I still don't see where I fit in.'

'I felt we needed someone with practical knowledge of drilling, someone with the experience to deal with any emergencies.'

'You having trouble here?'

'Not yet, no . . . But it's my job to cover every eventuality. Now, let me introduce you to some of our senior staff.'

Sutton followed him back into central control. He brightened perceptibly when Sir Keith introduced him to Petra Williams. 'Say, maybe I could borrow you for a bit. You could show me around, rattle off a few letters . . .'

'I am Professor Stahlman's personal assistant,' said Petra Williams frostily. 'I am not a typist, and I am not available for borrowing. If you'll excuse me, Sir Keith?' She moved pointedly away.

Sutton grinned. 'I think I've just been snubbed!'

'Come and meet Professor Stahlman himself,' said Sir Keith diplomatically.

He led Sutton over to Stahlman, who accepted the introduction without enthusiasm. 'Another recruit to your crusade, Sir Keith?'

Sutton was puzzled, sensing the hostile undercurrent. 'What crusade is that?'

'The crusade to bring this project to a grinding halt. Sir Keith is a dedicated man, you see. Dedicated to stifling me with over-caution, and a swarm of experts and advisers. I'm drowning in them, Mr Sutton.'

Greg Sutton said hotly, 'Now hang on a minute, I didn't ask for this job – '

'How you came here is of no importance, Mr Sutton. The fact is you are here. We see them everywhere: experts on this, experts on that . . .' He gestured as a tall cloaked figure stalked into central control. 'Here's another of them!'

The Doctor came to a halt and stood beaming cheerfully

17

at Stahlman's glowering figure. 'Our liver playing us up again this morning, Professor?' And he went on his way.

Stahlman turned away with a snarl. He had already learned that there was little use in trying to bully the Doctor.

'Who's the gentleman in fancy dress?' whispered Sutton.

'Oh, that's the Doctor. A brilliant mind. We're lucky to have him as adviser. Let me introduce you.'

Sir Keith made yet more introductions, and Sutton and the Doctor shook hands. 'Welcome to the Inferno, Mr Sutton. What do you think of this project?'

'A bit early to say, Doctor. What about you?'

'For a start, I think certain people should pay a lot more attention to the warnings of this computer. Not that I'm wild about computers, mind you. But they are a tool, and it's stupid to have a tool and not use it.'

The Doctor moved over to one of the sub-consoles and began flicking switches. 'Power for my own little project,' he said mysteriously. 'Nice to have met you Mr Sutton.'

A little bemused, Sutton nodded and moved away with Sir Keith.

The Doctor made a few more adjustments to the console and then headed for the exit. On his way he passed close to Stahlman, who was studying a console, surrounded by a little group of technicians.

'All these so called experts and advisers,' Stahlman was saying loudly. 'A waste of valuable time and money!'

The Doctor paused for a moment, studying the readings on the console. He leaned over the shoulder of the technician at Stahlman's elbow and tapped a dial. 'I'd give that a touch more lateral compensation, old chap, or you'll blow the main condenser banks. Costs thousands to put that right – waste of valuable time and money.'

Leaving Stahlman seething behind him, the Doctor strolled happily away.

'I am rapidly losing patience with that man', muttered Stahlman. But the Doctor was gone.

The Doctor drove across the wasteland of scrubby grass, dirt roads, puddles and rusting railway-lines that separated the different buildings of the complex until he came to the ramshackle hut that he had appropriated for his own. It was a long one-storey building, some way from the centre of the complex but conveniently close to the main power lines – which suited the Doctor very well. A UNIT sentry, Private Wyatt, was patrolling by the hut as the Doctor drove up.

'Morning,' said the Doctor cheerfully. 'Any sign of that man Slocum yet?'

'No, sir. We're still looking.'

'Nasty business.'

'You'll be safe enough in your little hut, sir. Slocum hasn't got one of your funny gadgets.'

'Funny gadgets? Oh, I see . . .' The Doctor produced his sonic screwdriver and operated it. The double doors at the end of the hut swung open. 'It's only a door handle,' said the Doctor mildly. He drove inside the hut, and the doors closed behind him.

Private Wyatt grinned, and resumed his patrol.

The long hut served the Doctor as office, laboratory, and also as a garage for Bessie.

The central laboratory portion was almost completely filled by a free-standing many-sided control console. This was the console from the TARDIS control room which the Doctor had disconnected, had transported down to the project, and re-connected, quite illicitly, to the nuclear generator.

Liz Shaw, the Doctor's assistant, was checking over the cables that connected the console to the power lines that ran so conveniently close to the hut.

She was a serious-looking girl with reddish-brown hair. She wore a severely cut blue jacket, a rather incongruously frivolous-looking mini-skirt, and a bright red blouse.

Liz Shaw was a scientist of some distinction in her own right. She had been conscripted from her post at Cambridge into UNIT some time ago, at first very much against her will. However, since then, the arrival of the Doctor had made the job fascinating, baffling and infuriating, all at the same time.

Liz looked up and smiled as the Doctor jumped out of the

19

car. 'How are things at central control?'

'Usual friction between Stahlman and Sir Keith.'

'Did you see the Brigadier?'

'Yes. There's been a murder, Liz. Dreadful business. A murder without a motive – on top of everything else. Still, we must get on with our work.' The Doctor began checking over the TARDIS console.

'You're determined to go ahead with this trial run?'

'I must, Liz. You see, without the TARDIS, I'm lost. A stranger in a foreign land, a shipwrecked mariner.'

'When do you want to make the run?'

'In just a few minutes' time.'

'Why the sudden rush?'

'We've been over this routine often enough, Liz. You know what to do?'

'Yes.'

'Take your position then, and switch the power through when I give the word.'

'I wish you'd think again, Doctor.'

'Liz, *please*!'

Reluctantly Liz took her position by the Doctor's improvised power-relay.

'Right,' said the Doctor. 'When I signal give me first-stage power, then the full burst just a fraction later.'

'Suppose it doesn't work?'

'I'll think of something – I hope!'

Liz threw a switch, and the TARDIS console began humming with power. There was a faint, wheezing groaning sound . . .

The main switch-room of the nuclear reactor was deep inside the low concrete bunker. It contained the console that fed power from the reactor through into main control, where it was monitored and passed on to the drill-head itself.

Bromley, one of the power-technicians, was using a wall telephone to report to main control. 'All readings normal here. No peaks at all.' He didn't see the strange twisted shape looming up behind him.

'Standing by, Doctor,' reported Liz.

The Doctor made a final check of the console. His plan was simple. He hoped, by a sudden massive power surge, to over-ride the cut-outs with which his Time Lord superiors had restricted the movements of the TARDIS. 'Right, Liz. Give me first-stage power.'

Liz fed more power through the console. The throbbing increased and the console began to vibrate, lights flashing furiously on the different control panels. The Doctor darted from one to the other, adjusting and compensating. 'Full power, Liz!'

The TARDIS console juddered furiously. The centre column rose and fell.

In the reactor switch-room, Bromley lay sprawled out on the floor.

A hunched, deformed figure was bent over the controls, pushing up the power to maximum output . . .

The TARDIS console was vibrating furiously now, as if it would shake itself to pieces.

The Doctor hung on frantically, shouting, 'Too much power, Liz. Too much power!'

'I can't cut back, Doctor,' shouted Liz. 'The circuits are overloading and locked!'

Suddenly the Doctor and the TARDIS console shuddered and disappeared before her eyes.

The Doctor found himself clinging to the console turning over and over, swept up in the blackness of limbo . . .

Liz worked frantically to pull back the power switches, but they were locked on maximum. She looked around frantically, snatched up a heavy, metal, office chair and slammed it into the Doctor's power relay.

It exploded in a shower of sparks, and the Doctor and the TARDIS console reappeared. The Doctor was upside down.

Liz ran over to him. 'Doctor, are you all right?'

The Doctor sorted himself out and patted and prodded himself. Everything seemed to be there. 'I'm still a bit dizzy, but I seem to be in one piece.'

'Where did you go?'

'I seemed to be in some kind of limbo. There was a barrier I couldn't break through. I need another trial run, Liz.'

'After all that?'

'*Because* of all that! I wonder where I was – and where I was going?'

Suddenly the electronic howl of an alarm rang through the complex.

'The drill-head,' said Liz. 'Something's happened!'

The whole of central control was being shaken by the terrible vibrating roar that was coming from the drill area.

Petra was shouting into a wall phone. 'Can you clear me a line, please? I must get through to the main switch-room. This is an emergency!'

Stahlman came running into central control. He stopped when he saw the heavy metal shield descending across the mouth of the tunnel that led to the drill-head area.

He turned on Sir Keith. 'Did you order that shield to be lowered? Why?'

'This is a Red-One emergency, Professor,' shouted Sir Keith.

'Is it? I haven't said so yet,' said Stahlman arrogantly. He grabbed the nearest technician by the arm. 'Get that fire shield up again – now!'

'But Professor – ' protested Sir Keith.

'Anything that happens in this area is my responsibility,' screamed Stahlman. '*Anything!* Is that clear?'

'Aren't you going to order the power shut off?'

'And stop the drill?' Stahlman saw Petra coming towards him. 'Have you contacted the reactor yet?'

'I can't get any answer, Professor.'

'You must get an answer.'

Sir Keith turned to Sutton. 'The man is obsessed. Why can't he just stop the drill till the emergency is over?'

Sutton shook his head. 'Not at this depth. You'd never get it going again, the drill bit would just seize up, lock into the strata. You'll have to abandon the bore.'

Suddenly Sir Keith understood. Stahlman would risk

22

anything – *anything* – rather than do that.

Stahlman snatched the phone from Petra's hands. 'I will talk to them. You go and see if they have the coolant flowing.'

Obediently Petra headed for the tunnel. Suddenly she found Greg Sutton blocking her way. He took her arm. 'I wouldn't go in there if I were you. The pressure could blow the roof right off the building.'

'I'm well aware what can happen, Mr Sutton, but I've got a job to do.'

She pulled free and ran down the tunnel.

Liz Shaw and the Doctor arrived at central control at the same time as the Brigadier and Sergeant Benton.

The Brigadier looked round appalled. 'What's happening?'

'There's been a sudden power surge, Brigadier. They must have gone mad at the reactor . . .'

Suddenly the Doctor broke off, remembering that there was indeed a madman on the loose. He looked at the Brigadier. 'Have you found Slocum yet?'

'No,' said the Brigadier grimly. 'But one of my men has been found murdered.'

'Where?'

'On the waste ground behind the reactor.'

The Doctor looked round and saw Stahlman at the telephone. 'Professor, we think we know what is happening here . . .'

'Stop wasting my time, Doctor,' snarled Stahlman.

'I was wrong about you, Professor,' said the Doctor. 'It isn't just your liver, it's your general disposition! Come on, Brigadier.'

They hurried from the control room.

Petra ran out of the tunnel and found Stahlman, still shouting in vain into the telephone. 'Professor, the coolant controls are jammed with the heat!'

Abandoning the phone, Stahlman headed for the tunnel.

Petra followed, passing Greg Sutton on the way. 'Well, Mr Sutton, the roof's still on!' She smiled sweetly at him. 'Aren't you rather nervous for an oil man?'

23

'I'm not nervous,' said Sutton bluntly. 'I'm terrified. I know what can happen in there, and you don't. You're not brave, you're just plain stupid.'

Petra said defiantly. 'Professor Stahlman knows what's happening. He'll deal with it.'

She hurried down the tunnel after Stahlman. For some reason, Greg Sutton found himself following her.

In the drill-head area, terrified technicians were wrestling with heat-jammed coolant controls, while Stahlman screamed frantically, 'Come on! Come *on*!'

Greg Sutton was no stranger to situations like this. Looking round he spotted the main coolant valve. A technician was wrestling in vain with the pressure wheel.

Sutton went over and moved the man gently aside. 'All right, old son, let's have a go at that. Soon have it under control.' He gripped the metal wheel and heaved steadily, muscles bulging under the linen safari suit. Slowly, very slowly, the wheel began to turn.

The Doctor and the Brigadier hurried into the switch-room, followed by Private Wyatt, who had been scooped up on the way. The Doctor took in the situation at a glance. While the Brigadier went to examine the crumpled body of the technician, the Doctor grabbed the main power lever and began pulling it back. He snatched his hand away – the lever was hot. Suddenly an inner door was flung open and a ghastly shape lurched towards them.

3

Mutant

The shambling figure advanced towards them. It was the hands that the Doctor noticed first – terrible misshapen, twisted claws, covered with hair. The face was a ghastly livid green, the eyes red and savage. If the feet were as distorted as the hands, thought the Doctor, it would account for the creature's awkward shuffling gait.

More curious than frightened, the Doctor took a step towards Slocum, who snarled and lashed out at him with a clawed hand. Hastily the Doctor jumped back. 'Don't move, Brigadier. Don't antagonise him.'

The Doctor, the Brigadier and the soldier stood motionless.

Slocum confronted them, his head swinging to and fro. Suddenly he *screeched* . . .

Sutton stepped back, mopping his streaming forehead. 'She ought to calm down now the coolant's flowing.'

'Thank you, Mr Sutton,' said Stahlman grudgingly. He checked an instrument panel. 'There is still far too much power coming from the reactor.'

'I think the Doctor went over there to deal with it,' said Petra.

The Doctor edged towards the controls.

Slocum snarled . . .

'Nothing to be frightened of, old chap,' said the Doctor soothingly.

Seeing that Slocum's attention seemed to be fixed on the Doctor, Private Wyatt began edging round to one side, his finger on the trigger of his rifle.

The phone on the wall began ringing insistently.

On the other end of the phone Petra said, 'There's still no reply.'

'What do those fools think they are doing?' snarled Stahlman. He snatched the phone. 'Hello! Hello?'

Private Wyatt snapped his fingers to attract the Doctor's attention. The Doctor glanced quickly at him, and Wyatt signalled with his eyes that the Doctor should move aside. The Doctor nodded almost imperceptibly, and began edging to one side.

Slocum screeched furiously, following him with his eyes.

Slowly Wyatt raised his rifle . . .

The Doctor jumped suddenly to one side, and Private Wyatt took aim. Immediately Slocum sprang to the attack. Private Wyatt fired as he had been trained to do, two shots close together, two bullets in the heart. Slocum kept on coming, grappling with Wyatt and hurling him to one side. Then he staggered back, leaning against the wall, snarling with rage and pain. He glared wildly at them for a moment, and then slid slowly to the floor.

The Brigadier advanced cautiously towards the body.

'Don't touch him,' snapped the Doctor. 'Look at the wall where he slid down. It's scorched!'

The Brigadier examined the scorch-mark with astonishment, while the Doctor picked up Wyatt's rifle and used it to thrust back the power lever. When the job was completed, he became aware that the phone was still ringing. He picked it up.

He heard the tinny voice of Stahlman screeching at him from the other end of the line.

'Oh, it's you,' said the Doctor wearily. 'It's all right, Professor, we've dealt with the matter ourselves.'

Private Wyatt was sitting up, a strange, dazed expression on his face . . .

In the drill-head area things were calming down. The alarm lights blinked off one by one and the howl of the siren died away.

26

Greg Sutton heaved a sigh of relief. 'Well done, everybody. I'll have a new medal struck, Order of the Turkish Bath.'

Professor Stahlman made the same announcement in more formal tones. 'The emergency has been contained. Return to normal duties.'

'We contained it by the skin of our teeth,' said Sutton quietly. 'Next time we may not be so lucky.'

The main operation was not at fault,' snapped Stahlman. 'Those idiots at the reactor boosted the power too high.'

'So it was an accident. They happen, and you have to allow for them, and take precautions . . .'

'I refuse to make allowances for incompetence, Mr Sutton,' said Stahlman loftily, and turned away.

Sutton caught Petra's eye. 'Is that man completely nuts?'

'No, I don't think so. Thanks for all your help, Mr Sutton.'

He took her arm. 'Listen, call me Greg. And if you really are grateful, there's something you can do for me.'

Petra gave him a suspicious look. 'Such as?'

'I've got one or two ideas – about safety in the drill-head area. Stahlman listens to you, and if you could convince him I'm talking sense . . .'

The Doctor was examining Slocum's body, though he was careful not to touch it. He looked up. 'Both bullets right through the heart, Brigadier.'

'And he was alive and moving, for several minutes.'

'Abnormal resistance, abnormal strength,' muttered the Doctor. 'And that's not all . . .'

Sergeant Benton came into the room. 'Medics are on their way, sir.'

The Doctor said, 'Tell them they'd better not touch the body for a while – it's radiating a good deal of heat.'

'The man's dead, Doctor,' protested the Brigadier.

'Heat, Brigadier. Like the wrench that killed the technician. Like this control lever here.'

The Brigadier shook his head disbelievingly. 'What about these two, Doctor?'

Private Wyatt and the technician Bromley were both

sitting slumped against the wall. They were strangely quiet, almost as if drugged, their eyes wide and staring.

The Doctor looked curiously at them. 'They don't seem to have any major injuries. Could be the effects of shock, perhaps.' He leaned forward. 'Wyatt? Private Wyatt?'

Wyatt stared blankly ahead of him, and made no reply.

The Doctor and the Brigadier were on an iron platform, part of one of the great metal cooling towers that dominated the complex. Far below them, soldiers and technicians went about their affairs like busy ants. Lorries drove to and fro like toys, and on the edge of the complex a toy-like supply train chugged into the distance.

The Brigadier looked round, confident that from such a vantage point they could not possibly be overheard. 'Look, Doctor I need some answers. Exactly what did happen to Slocum?'

'A retrogressive mutation of the body cells, I think.'

'I don't understand.'

'Neither do I really, not yet.'

'He seemed to be turning into some sort of animal.'

'Yes. But the process was relatively slow, and it was by no means complete.'

The Brigadier said wearily, 'I'm going to have the devil of a job keeping this quiet.'

The Doctor stared out over the landscape. 'But why . . . Why wasn't the process completed?'

'That screeching he was making. Have you ever heard anything like it before, Doctor?'

'Yes, I have as a matter of fact.'

'Where?'

'Krakatoa in the Sundra Straits – during the eruption of 1883.'

'Doctor, are you telling me that there's some link between what happened to Slocum, and a volcanic eruption in Krakatoa?'

'There could be.'

The Brigadier gave him a despairing look, and fell silent. The Doctor was silent too, thinking about Krakatoa. Some of the natives believed that the volcano had a kind of evil spirit – that it was alive . . .

Benton climbed the ladder on to the platform. 'Sir, Private Wyatt and that technician, Bromley. They've disappeared.'

'They've what?'

'They both cleared off, sir, before the medics could get a look at them. We all thought they were too ill to move.'

Almost relieved to be faced with a purely practical problem, the Brigadier said briskly, 'Come on, Sergeant, we've got to find them.'

The two soldiers clattered off down the ladder, and the Doctor was left to himself. But not for long.

He heard a scraping sound above his head, and glancing upwards he saw a distorted figure shuffling along the catwalk that formed a sort of bridge between this tower and the next. The figure wore army uniform, but there was something very odd about the face – and about the hands. It was Private Wyatt . . .

'Wyatt!' shouted the Doctor. 'Wyatt, come back!' He ran to the ladder and began climbing up towards the catwalk. By the time he reached it, the shambling figure was nowhere in sight. The Doctor moved cautiously along the catwalk. On the other side he saw an access ladder, leading to a platform like the one he had just left. He slid nimbly down it, looked around . . . and then Wyatt lurched towards him from around the side of the tower.

The Doctor studied him cautiously. The terrible change that had overtaken Slocum had affected Wyatt too, though it was far more advanced. The eyes had the same savage red glare and the face was a terrible livid green. The hands were already crooked into claws, and the Doctor saw with astonishment that the tattered battle-dress jacket was beginning to smoulder.

Heat, thought the Doctor. The mutation was somehow connected with heat . . . it produced the most incredible amount of heat.

The Doctor backed away. 'Listen to me, Wyatt, you're sick. You need help . . .'

It was all over in seconds. Wyatt made a clumsy rush, swinging his rifle like a club. The Doctor leaped aside and

29

Wyatt pitched over the rail, crashing to the ground far below.

The Doctor went to the rail and looked down at the sprawled body. Already UNIT soldiers were running towards it. The Doctor leaned over the rail. 'Don't touch him,' he called. 'Whatever you do, don't touch him.' He turned from the rail and hurried towards the ladder that led to the ground.

After a few moments, another shambling figure shuffled around the edge of the tower. It was Bromley. His skin had a greenish pallor and his hands were crooked into claws . . .

4

The Slime

Stahlman was checking instrument-readings in the drill-head area. He looked up as Petra approached. 'According to my calculations, Petra, I can now increase the drilling rate by twelve per cent without adverse effects. This will advance the time of penetration of the Earth's crust by nearly five hours.'

Petra wasn't really listening. 'Can you come at·once please, Professor? There's something you should see in central control.'

When they emerged from the tunnel they found Sir Keith Gold, Greg Sutton and Liz Shaw gathered around a laboratory trolley upon which rested a large metal box. Beside the trolley there stood a masked and gauntleted laboratory technician.

Stahlman surveyed the little group without enthusiasm. 'Well?'

Sir Keith nodded to the technician, who opened the metal box and took out a thick glass jar. It was filled with a glutinous green slime, which seemed shot with little sparks of white-hot energy. It seethed and bubbled as if alive.

Sir Keith said quietly, 'They've been getting traces of this stuff in number 2 output pipe for some hours. Now it's beginning to come up in greater quantities.'

The Doctor and the Brigadier came into central control and joined the group.

Stahlman studied the substance curiously. 'Analysis report?'

'None. So far it defies analysis.'

'Impossible. Since it exists, it can be analysed.' Stahlman touched the jar and snatched his finger away. 'We'll just have to wait till it cools down.'

'I doubt if it will cool down,' said the Doctor thoughtfully.

Stahlman swung round on him. 'Who the devil asked you?'

'Just venturing an opinion,' said the Doctor blandly.

'Based on what?'

'Krakatoa, actually.'

The Brigadier stepped forward. 'Professor Stahlman, I must talk to you on a matter of great urgency.'

'Not now,' said Stahlman, and turned away.

'I'm afraid I must insist, sir.'

Stahlman whirled round. 'Then talk to Sir Keith. He has time for talking, I do not.'

He turned to move off, but the Brigadier barred his way. 'In the last few hours, Professor, two men have died in this establishment – died violently. I must talk to you both in my office – now.'

For once Stahlman recognised a will as strong as his own. 'Very well.'

The Brigadier looked at Sir Keith, who said hurriedly, 'Yes, of course. Lead the way, Brigadier.'

The Brigadier led Stahlman and Sir Keith out of the room.

'I examined that stuff in the labs, Doctor,' said Liz. 'What do you make of it?'

The Doctor peered thoughtfully at the jar. 'I wish I could hear it. I wonder if it screeches.'

Liz gave him a puzzled look. 'And there's something else, Doctor. I think you ought to come and have a look at the data on the main computer.'

'Something worrying, Liz?'

'Something downright frightening.'

The Brigadier was getting nowhere with his meeting.

Stahlman listened impatiently to his account of the recent mysterious events. 'I'm sorry, Brigadier, but this matter has nothing to do with the technical side of the operation. It is not my responsibility.'

'The Doctor thinks there is a direct connection – '

'The Doctor has no authority here.'

'Come now,' protested Sir Keith. 'His work on initial

stress was invaluable. You had a team of mathematicians working on that particular problem for a month, and the Doctor gave you the answer in ten minutes.'

'That is not the point – '

The Brigadier raised his voice. 'Professor Stahlman, please! I am still waiting for answers to my particular problems.'

'As you say, Brigadier, they are your problems. Deal with them as you see fit!'

The Doctor marched into the office. 'A question! Isn't anyone going to take any notice of that computer?'

'What are you jabbering about?' asked Stahlman wearily. 'That computer is over-sensitive.'

'You talk about the thing as though it were your maiden aunt!'

'I do not need the computer, Doctor,' said Stahlman arrogantly. 'It is of no interest to me. My own calculations are more specific and more accurate.'

'Professor Stahlman, allow me to tell you something that should be of vital interest to you.'

'Yes?'

The Doctor drew himself up to his full height, glared down at Stahlman and shouted, 'You, sir, are a nitwit.'

Stahlman rose and walked towards the door, almost colliding with Petra as she ran in.

'Professor, come quickly! Something's happening to that stuff in the jar.'

The substance in the glass jar was seething and bubbling and hissing. Petra said, 'I think it's going to shatter it!'

Suddenly the green slime began forcing its way past the seal of the glass jar's stopper. A few drops trickled down the side.

Before anyone could stop him, Professor Stahlman snatched up the jar, put it back inside the shielded box and slammed the lid shut.

The Doctor sighed. 'I wouldn't have touched that if I were you!'

Stahlman turned to the lab technician. 'Have that stuff frozen immediately!' He glared round the group. 'Now, can

33

we all get back to work? The entertainment is over!'

Suddenly Stahlman rubbed at his hand, which seemed to have been burned by the drops of glowing slime.

'Are you all right?' asked the Brigadier.

'Of course.'

'Then perhaps we could continue our discussion.'

'I don't think there is any point, Brigadier. As far as I am concerned, everything has already been said.'

The Brigadier controlled himself with an effort. 'Thank you for your co-operation, Professor Stahlman.'

'But what about the computer, Professor?' persisted Sir Keith. 'You can't just ignore it.'

'I prefer to use my own judgement. I have spent eleven years working on this project, and I know more about it than any machine.'

'I hope you do,' said the Doctor grimly. 'The message of the computer is perfectly clear. It advises that drilling be stopped immediately. It's warning you of danger. Look at it, man, are you blind?'

Stahlman turned away. 'The computer, as I have said, is inaccurate.'

'Oh, please yourself, sir!' said the Doctor explosively. 'I've done the best I can to convince you. I may as well get back to my own work.'

It was the moment Stahlman had been waiting for. 'You may find that rather difficult, Doctor. This project cannot supply you with any more power.'

'And why not?'

'The entire output of the reactor is needed for the project. I intend to accelerate the drilling rate by twelve per cent.'

Stahlman turned to a technician. 'Shut off the power supply to the Doctor's hut immediately. It is not to be re-connected in any circumstances.'

As the technician moved to obey, the Doctor said bitterly, 'That, sir, is an incredibly childish and petty action.'

Stahlman smiled. 'Will you excuse me? Petra, come with me please.'

They moved away.

Sir Keith looked helplessly at the Doctor. 'I'm sorry, Doctor.'

'So am I, Sir Keith. So am I.'

In the drilling area, Stahlman stood surveying the central drill-head with evident satisfaction. 'We shall start the acceleration in exactly twenty-five minutes' time. That will make the time of penetration-zero exactly – forty-nine hours from now.'

Petra made a note on her clipboard. 'Forgive me, Professor Stahlman, but shouldn't you at least consider what the others are saying?'

'If I had listened to others, Petra, this project would never have got started. If I listen now, it will never be completed. Have all systems modified to the new programming immediately.'

The Doctor was about to return to his hut when he saw Petra Williams move over to the main power relay console. 'Mr Phillips, Professor Stahlman has decided to make some modifications to the drilling schedule. Will you join us please?'

As Petra and Phillips moved into the tunnel, the Doctor saw his chance and seized it.

'Liz, I want you to go back to the hut for me, there's a good girl. Just check those trigamma circuits on the console, will you?'

'Very well.' Puzzled, Liz moved away.

The Doctor drifted casually over to the main power relay, glanced round, and set to work. A minute or two later, he straightened up, and moved away.

He was about to leave central control when he saw Stahlman come out of the tunnel and wander across to the computer with a deliberate vagueness curiously like the Doctor's own. Then he moved towards the computer console. The Doctor had a sudden powerful suspicion that Professor Stahlman was up to no good.

His suspicions were confirmed when Stahlman opened a panel in the console, swiftly removed a circuit, slipped it into his pocket and strode away.

'Jumping Jehosophat,' thought the Doctor. 'The man's sabotaging his own computer!'

Professor Stahlman hurried for the nearest door, which as it happened led to the Brigadier's empty office. He took the circuit from his pocket, laid it on the desk, and looked round for something heavy. Snatching up an ebony ruler he raised it high. He was about to smash it down on the circuit when a voice said, 'I wouldn't do that, Professor.' The Doctor was watching him from the doorway.

'You would be well advised to mind your own business, Doctor.' Stahlman grabbed the circuit with his other hand.

'That computer is a threat to you, isn't it? It could prove you wrong. Now – give me that circuit.'

Stahlman took a step forward as if to obey. Then raising the heavy ebony ruler, he brought it slashing down towards the Doctor's head.

The Doctor shot out a long arm and jabbed two bony fingers into a point just below Stahlman's collarbone. Stahlman froze, the ruler suspended in mid-air. He was a powerfully built man, in a tremendous rage, but somehow he was quite unable to move a muscle. He just stood there, his face gradually turning purple with anger.

The Brigadier appeared in the doorway to his office and halted, appalled. 'May I ask what you're doing, Doctor?'

'Venusian aikido, Brigadier. Very effective. Of course if you hold it too long, the subject remains permanently paralysed.'

'Then I suggest you let Professor Stahlman go.'

'Certainly!' The Doctor removed his fingers, and Stahlman slumped forwards onto the desk.

'Thank you,' said the Brigadier. 'Now perhaps someone will explain what's going on here?'

The Doctor said, 'Well, Professor – shall I tell him or will you?'

Stahlman straightened up. 'Brigadier, I want this man expelled from the complex immediately. That is an order.' He turned and left the office.

The Doctor hurried after him.

'What do you think you're doing?' called the Brigadier.

'Don't start asking silly questions, Brigadier. Just follow me!'

They followed Stahlman out into central control. 'Just a

'moment, Professor,' called the Doctor. 'We need some answers from you.'

Stahlman swung round. 'This man is trying to sabotage my project, Brigadier.'

'Oh am I?' said the Doctor indignantly. 'Just be good enough to show me what you've got in your left-hand pocket.'

Stahlman glared indignantly at him.

The Brigadier said apologetically, 'Profesor – if you wouldn't mind?'

Stahlman snatched out the contents of his left-hand jacket pocket and slammed them on top of the console, and turned the pocket inside out. He did the same with the right-hand pocket.

The Doctor and the Brigadier looked at the collection of objects. Keys, a handkerchief, a notebook, small change, a penknife . . . nothing but the usual everyday things that anyone might carry.

'Satisfied?' snarled Stahlman. 'Now get that man out of my sight!' He crammed his possessions back into his pockets and walked away.

The Brigadier looked at the Doctor. 'Well?'

'I tell you he had a micro-circuit in that pocket, Brigadier.'

'It isn't there now, is it?'

Suddenly the busy whirring and chattering of the computer banks faltered. Slowly they came to a halt.

The Doctor nodded towards the computer. 'You see? It's packing up already.'

Before the Brigadier could reply, the Doctor stalked off.

An agitated group of technicians had gathered around the computer, and the Brigadier moved to join them. Taking advantage of the confusion, Stahlman slipped back towards the Brigadier's office. Just under the desk lay a tiny gleaming object – the missing micro-circuit, still lying where Stahlman had dropped it. Viciously Stahlman ground it to powder with the heel of his shoe.

Liz Shaw was still working on the TARDIS console when the Doctor marched into the hut, his face grim and determined.

'Find any damage to the circuits, Liz?'

'A couple of by-pass circuits had burned out, but I replaced them.'

'Good, good.'

'Still, with the power cut off we're just wasting our time, aren't we? I mean, you won't be able to make any more trial runs – I'm glad to say!'

'It wasn't the console that was to blame, Liz. If it hadn't been for that sudden unexpected surge of power . . .'

Liz smiled. 'Well, maybe. But I'm afraid we'll never know for sure.'

'Liz, do you think you could do me a favour? Just slip back to central control and feed this into the spare computer bank.' He handed her a sheaf of notes.

Liz glanced at them. 'Epsilon co-ordinates? You usually work those out in your head.'

'Yes, but you see – well, to be honest I'm a little tired.'

'All right, Doctor,' said Liz sympathetically. She took the co-ordinates and headed for the door.

'Allow me,' said the Doctor. He produced his sonic screwdriver and operated the remote control on the door. It rose, and Liz went outside.

As soon as she was gone, the Doctor sprang to life, making a number of complex adjustments on his power transformer. It seemed almost as if he was working against time.

Liz came into central control. A great commotion was going on around the computer. She went over to the Brigadier, who was standing on the edge of the group looking baffled. 'What's happening?'

'The computer appears to have broken down.'

Liz waved her sheaf of notes. 'The Doctor will have to do his calculations in his head after all.'

The Brigadier said slowly, 'The Doctor sent you? But – he was here when the computer first broke down. He sent you on a wild goose chase, Miss Shaw.'

They looked at each other for a moment and then Liz said, 'Come on, Brigadier!'

The Doctor stepped back and examined his work. It was

more difficult to make the test run without Liz to help – but it wasn't impossible. All he needed was the incorporation of a simple remote-control device to feed the power through in stages.

He switched on and dashed back to the TARDIS console. There was a steadily rising hum of power and the console began to shudder and vibrate. There was a wheezing, groaning sound. The Doctor gripped the edge of the console with all his might. Suddenly console and Doctor began flicking in and out of reality.

In central control the lights suddenly began dimming and brightening again.

Petra hurried up to Stahlman, who was studying the power readings in astonishment. 'What's happening, Professor?'

'Someone's using extra power.' Stahlman smashed a fist down onto the nearest console. 'It's him! It's that Doctor!' He rushed to the power console, and saw, as he had expected, that the power to the Doctor's hut had been re-connected. Stahlman grabbed for a cut-out switch and pulled it back.

The Brigadier and Liz ran up to the open door of the hut, which was filled with the roar of power. They saw the shuddering console, the Doctor hanging on desperately . . .

Suddenly the Doctor, the console and even the little yellow car shimmered and faded out of existence. The roar of the power cut out. The hut was silent – and empty. The Doctor, the TARDIS console and Bessie had all three disappeared.

5

Dimension of Terror

Liz ran to the power transformer and flicked desperately at the controls. 'Nothing – it's dead. Stahlman must have cut off the power again. Wherever the Doctor is, he's trapped!'

The Brigadier said, 'I think you'd better let me know what's been going on, Miss Shaw.'

'I'll tell you on the way over to central control.'

By the time they reached the main control room, the Brigadier knew all about the Doctor's experiments with the Stahlman project's power, and his previous temporary disappearance. He would have a number of extremely cutting things to say to the Doctor when he returned – if he returned.

The roar of the drill seemed louder and more frantic in the control centre now. It was obvious that Stahlman had resumed the accelerated drilling.

He was studying the power readings with evident satisfaction, when the Brigadier and Liz approached.

'Professor Stahlman!'

'Not now, Brigadier.'

'I want you to re-connect the power to the Doctor's hut.'

'Don't be ridiculous!'

'Professor Stahlman, the Doctor has disappeared!'

'Excellent! For once he's done as he was told.'

'You don't understand,' said Liz desperately. 'He was engaged in an experiment, and you switched off the power at a crucial moment. You've got to restore it.'

'My dear young woman, I denied the Doctor a power source when he was here – I'm scarcely likely to restore it now that he's gone.'

Sir Keith tried to help. 'Professor Stahlman, be reasonable.'

'I have been more than reasonable, ever since this project began. I've tolerated your experts and advisers. But now we have accelerated the drilling programme, and I will not be disturbed further.'

'You had no right to accelerate the programme without proper consultation with the Ministry.'

'I have every right.'

'Then I'm sorry, but I shall have to appeal to the Minister.'

'Please do. I can tell you exactly what he'll say. "This project is vital to the country's industrial future. We must have a new power source – and Stahlman is the only one who can get it for us!" '

Liz could see that the fate of the Doctor had been forgotten. 'Please, we must have the power supply reconnected.'

'The matter is closed,' said Stahlman coldly. 'Under no circumstances will any power be reconnected to the Doctor's hut.' He walked away.

'What exactly has happened to the Doctor?' asked Sir Keith.

The Brigadier hesitated. 'He's vanished.'

'We're afraid he may be in danger,' said Liz.

Sir Keith said worriedly, 'I'm afraid we may all be in danger – unless we can get the drilling rate slowed down.'

'Will you go to London, sir?' asked the Brigadier.

'There's no alternative. Someone's got to control Stahlman.'

'Do you think they'll listen to you?'

'I very much doubt it. Stahlman was right. They believe he's the only one who can make this project succeed. I'm just a figurehead. But I shall go and try, just as soon as I've cleared my work.'

Liz frowned. 'Surely you ought to go now – at once?'

'My dear Miss Shaw, the project is reaching a crucial stage. If Stahlman can find any chance to accuse me of negligence, he will – and who will believe me then?'

Stahlman stood staring at the drill-head mechanism, his eyes blazing. He glanced down at his left hand, and saw a great stain spreading across the skin. He took a pair of white gloves from his pocket and put them on.

Petra came up to him in time to see what was happening. 'Are you all right, Professor?'

'Perfectly.'

'Hadn't you better get a doctor to take a look at that hand?'

'*I am perfectly all right!*' He became calmer. 'Now, may I suggest that we continue with our work?'

In central control the Brigadier was saying, 'I'm sorry, Miss Shaw, there's nothing more we can do.'

'What about the Doctor? You don't seem very worried.'

'Professor Stahlman seems determined to blow us all to kingdom come, the Doctor has vanished, and I have a number of unsolved murders on my hands. I promise you, Miss Shaw, I'm extremely worried!'

For what seemed a very long time the Doctor had been whirling helplessly in some kind of limbo, a place where not only time and space but the fabric of reality itself seemed to be distorted. He felt as if he was being split off, so that there were not one but ten, a hundred, a thousand, a million Doctors – with a million TARDIS consoles and a million Bessies to go with them.

Suddenly he hit the ground with a jolt, and opened his eyes. He was back in his hut. The place was the same, and yet – it was different. Wonderingly, the Doctor looked around him. To begin with it was neat – an unlikely state of affairs where the Doctor was concerned. He liked a bit of clutter.

The hut – this hut – was fanatically, meticulously tidy, like an army barrack room on the eve of an inspection. In fact the whole place had a distinctly military air. The wall shelves, that had formerly been piled high with the Doctor's books and papers and journals and scientific instruments, now held nothing but rows of metal boxes, labelled according to some kind of code. Walls and floor were spotless. There was a large poster fixed to the wall beside the door. It showed a thin-faced rather cruel-looking man with a neatly trimmed moustache. Beneath the picture there was a slogan – 'Unity is Strength'. Beneath it was a symbol – three arrows radiating from a common hub.

'Who's been messing about with my workshop?' muttered the Doctor indignantly. ' "Unity is Strength" indeed!' He fished out his sonic screwdriver, and tried to operate the remote control on the door. Nothing happened. Puzzled, the Doctor pushed the door open and went outside.

He stood looking around him, even more puzzled than before. Like the inside of the hut, the whole landscape had been – tidied up. There was none of the sprawl and clutter of the old refinery, no rackety lorries and scruffy old goods trains. Instead, there was a neat complex of tidily arranged buildings, with here and there a few military-looking vehicles, marked with the three-arrow symbol. The cooling towers and steel gantries were still there, but they had been cleaned and painted and polished until they shone.

The Doctor scratched his head, and went back inside the hut, noticing as he did so that there was a three-arrow symbol on the door.

Then he climbed into Bessie, started her up and drove away.

Before he had gone very far, a shot spanged off Bessie's bonnet. The Doctor turned and saw that a strangely uniformed soldier in a black forage cap had appeared from behind some buildings.

'Hey!' yelled the Doctor indignantly, 'What do you think you're doing?'

The man raised his rifle and fired again.

The Doctor put his foot down and sped away.

It was the beginning of a kind of nightmare. As he drove along the now neatly concreted access roads, more and more soldiers appeared. They all wore black forage caps and shoulder-flashes with the three-arrow symbol. More important still, they were all armed, and they were all shooting at him.

The Doctor sped along between the buildings, spinning and skidding round corners, trying in vain to avoid or out-pace his attackers. He drove out of the paved area and onto a kind of wasteland at the edge of the compound. Suddenly there was a massive wall topped with barbed wire looming up in front of him. No escape that way.

The Doctor slowed Bessie and made a quick U-turn – and as he did so a soldier came bounding towards him, fired and missed, and leaped onto the bonnet of the car. By now the Doctor was well under way. The soldier clung on desperately, clawing his way along the side of the car in a desperate attempt to reach the Doctor. As his hands reached out, the Doctor swung up one of his long legs, and shot it out, heaving the man from the car with a hearty kick. But there were other soldiers, an unending number of them . . .

Driving in a sort of fast zig-zag, the Doctor shot across the wasteland and drove down a little street, made up, he guessed, of the administration buildings. Soldiers appeared at the end of the street ahead of him. Looking around, the Doctor saw that there were more behind. The circle of his pursuers was closing in.

Abruptly the Doctor swung Bessie down the gap between two buildings, into a back alley lined with litter bins. When the soldiers came running up they saw the little car parked at an angle, with the Doctor nowhere in sight. They spread out and began to search.

When the search party had moved on, the lid of one of the huge litter bins slowly rose, revealing the head of the Doctor underneath. It wasn't the most dignified of hiding-places, thought the Doctor as he climbed out of the bin, but it was better than being shot.

But why was he being shot at? What on earth was going on here? If the TARDIS had taken him to some other time, or some other world, the Doctor would have understood. But to find himself in the same place – the same and yet so very different . . .

The Doctor looked round to get his bearings and saw that he wasn't very far from the metal cooling towers. Perhaps they would offer a better hiding-place. For the moment at least the way seemed clear, so the Doctor sprinted towards the nearest tower, swung himself up onto a metal ladder and began to climb.

He reached the platform that led to the catwalk that made

a bridge to the next tower, and paused to look down. He was very high up by now. He could see the soldiers running between the buildings like disturbed ants, and jeep-like military vehicles speeding to and fro with more armed men, and he could hear the wail of the alarm sirens. Whatever this place was, thought the Doctor, it had a very sensitive security system . . .

Suddenly the Doctor heard a low, primitive growl. He turned and saw a hideous figure shuffling across the platform towards him. It was Bromley, the man he had encountered once before; Bromley transformed into a ferocious beast by that same strange recessive mutation. The eyes glowed a fiery red, the hands were crooked savage claws, and the face was beginning to sprout coarse black hair. Bromley opened his mouth, and made an unearthly screeching sound.

With the strangest feeling that his life was somehow repeating itself, the Doctor backed away . . .

He looked round desperately for a weapon – and saw a fire-extinguisher clipped to the rail. It would probably hold CO_2 gas under pressure. The gas, when it emerged, would be intensely cold, and the mutants seemed to crave heat. Levelling the extinguisher, the Doctor pulled back the lever. A cloud of icy white vapour shot out, enveloping Bromley, who screeched and fell writhing to the ground.

Suddenly the Doctor heard a shout of 'There he is!' A bullet whistled close to his head.

The Doctor ran along the catwalk to the next tower and began to climb. Gasping, he pulled himself up onto the dome roof, and ran across to the other side. The ladder on the far side would take him back to the ground – and for the moment at least, he would be out of sight of the soldiers. But before he could reach it a shambling figure swarmed up the ladder and advanced towards him. It was another of the mutants – the Doctor recognised the distorted features of Private Wyatt, though the mutation was so far advanced that it was hard to tell.

The Doctor looked round – no handy fire-extinguisher this time. There was a section of metal piping by his feet. The Doctor snatched it up, and hurled it at the creature.

The mutant swept it aside with an angry snarl and

advanced on the Doctor, driving him back across the roof of the tower. The creature charged.

The Doctor leaped aside and the monster rushed past, cannoning into the guard rail at the edge of the tower.

Far below a soldier looked up, and spotted a silhouetted figure at the top of the tower. 'There he is, sir. He's on the tower!'

'Fire!' ordered the squad commander. 'Fire at will!'

The soldier raised his rifle.

The mutant swung round to confront the Doctor. It gave an unearthly screch and crouched as if to spring.

The Doctor prepared to dodge. But he knew he couldn't avoid the creature indefinitely. Not in this bare open space so high above the ground. Sooner or later those clawed hands would seize hold of him, and it would all be over.

The mutant screeched again, and a shot rang out. The creature staggered, spun round, and pitched headlong over the guard rail.

The Doctor ran to the rail and saw its body hurtling downwards, saw it thud into the ground, scattering the little knot of soldiers below. He turned and sprinted across the top of the tower to the ladder on the far side. Swinging himself over the side, he slid down the outer edges of the ladder like a fireman's pole, not bothering with the rungs. In an astonishingly short time he had reached the ground and was running for the shelter of a pile of scattered storage crates on the other side of the road.

As the Doctor crouched in hiding, considering his next move, he heard footsteps coming along the road. He peeped cautiously out of his hiding-place and saw a young woman marching towards him. She was strangely dressed and her hair was different, but the face was quite unmistakable.

'Liz!' called the Doctor delightedly. 'Liz!' He sprang out of hiding, just as she walked by. Slowly the young woman turned to face him. It was Liz Shaw all right, there was no doubt of that. But this Liz had hair that was black rather than reddish-brown. She wore a brown uniform, a severely tailored skirt and blouse. A leather belt around her waist held a holstered revolver.

The Doctor stared at her in astonishment. 'Liz – it's me!

Don't you recognise me? What's happened round here, have you all gone mad? And what are you doing in that ridiculous uniform?'

Cold eyes stared at him, with no sign of recognition. The girl drew her revolver and levelled it. 'Put your hands up!'

'Come on, Liz, a joke's a joke,' said the Doctor. He moved towards her.

She levelled the revolver at his head. 'Keep back!' Without taking her eyes from the Doctor's face, she drew a whistle from the top pocket of her uniform and blew it hard.

The whistle blast rang out shrilly, and within seconds there was the clatter of booted feet, as a squad of soldiers came running up.

She nodded towards the Doctor. 'Take him away!'

To his astonishment, the Doctor recognised the burly, strangely uniformed figure in charge of the squad. It was Sergeant Benton.

6

The Nightmare

Benton and the soldiers marched the Doctor to a military vehicle, its sides painted with the three-arrow symbol. He was thrust inside. Benton and the girl got in with him, and a soldier drove them the short distance across the compound to a neater, more military version of the drill tower and other buildings he had known on the Stahlman project.

The Doctor was pulled out of the vehicle and dragged through a more orderly central control, where white-uniformed technicians moved silently about their duties. Then he was shoved unceremoniously into an office.

The room was in darkness, except for the pool of light that came from a powerful desk lamp. A man was sitting in the chair behind the desk. He had swivelled the chair round so that he could consult a chart on the wall behind him. As the Doctor and the others entered he turned, and the light fell full on his face.

The Doctor found himself looking at his old friend Brigadier Alastair Lethbridge-Stewart. But it was a very different Brigadier. For a start the moustache was gone. Without it the Brigadier's mouth was thin-lipped and cruel. This Brigadier had a black patch over his left eye, a scar ran from the patch down to his jaw line. Yet somehow these changes were only superficial. The real change was in the spirit of the man. The lines of the face were harsh, and the eye cold. It was as if all the Brigadier's essential humanity had been suppressed. Only the harsher military qualities remained.

'Is this the man?' said the uniformed figure.

The Doctor stared at him in amazement. 'Brigadier! What are you doing in that get-up?'

Benton gave him a savage jab with his rifle-butt. 'Keep quiet!'

'You will find it unwise to be insolent,' said the man behind the desk. 'How did you gain entry to this establishment?'

'Look,' said the Doctor desperately. 'I *know* you . . . and you know me. Your name *is* Lethbridge-Stewart?'

The man seemed surprised. 'Yes.'

'*Brigadier* Lethbridge-Stewart.'

'*Brigade-Leader* Lethbridge-Stewart.'

'All right, Brigade-Leader, have it your own way.' The Doctor turned to the girl. 'And you're Liz Shaw?'

'I am Section-Leader Elizabeth Shaw.'

'And you're Sergeant Benton?'

'Platoon Under-Leader Benton.'

The Doctor sighed.

'How do you know our names?' demanded Section-Leader Shaw.

'You have been spying on this establishment,' accused the Brigade-Leader. 'What is your name?'

'My name? You want to know my name after all the years we've – '

The Doctor broke off, a terrible realisation sweeping over him. 'I'm beginning to understand what's happened . . . May I suggest that you just call me the Doctor?'

'Doctor? Doctor what?'

'John Smith?' said the Doctor hopefully.

'Smith. Yes, of course. And where do you come from Doctor *Smith*?'

The Doctor sighed. 'I'm afraid this is going to be the difficult bit.' He paused, wondering how to express his new understanding.

'Well?' snapped the Brigade-Leader impatiently.

'I come from a parallel space/time continuum.'

Section-Leader Shaw said, 'Obviously he is trying to confuse us, Leader.'

'Let me put it another way,' said the Doctor helpfully. 'I've been transported here from another universe which is running almost parallel to this one – with a few very important differences it seems.'

Section-Leader Shaw looked at her superior. 'He's mad.'

49

'No. I see what he's up to: he's trying to make us *think* he's mad.' He glared at the Doctor. 'Well, it won't work my friend.'

The Doctor turned to the woman. 'Even in this world, you're still Liz Shaw.'

'I am Section-Leader Elizabeth Shaw, yes.'

'Are you a scientist?'

'No. I am a security officer.'

'Fascinating. So many similarities, yet so many differences.'

'Enough of this!' shouted the Brigade-Leader. 'I want the truth.'

'Tell me, how far down is the shaft you're drilling here?'

'You see, Leader?' said Elizabeth Shaw. 'He is a spy!'

'And how's Professor Stahlman?' asked the Doctor cheerfully. 'Still having trouble with his liver? And what about Sir Keith? Now, there's a man who might understand.'

'What do you know about Sir Keith?'

'I know he's the Executive Director of this project. Yes, I should like to speak to Sir Keith very much.'

'Would you indeed?'

'Indeed I would! Or failing that, Professor Stahlman. He's an opinionated oaf, I know, but at least he's a scientist.'

'Very well,' said the Brigade-Leader unexpectedly.

Section-Leader Shaw was horrified. 'Are you really taking this man to see the Director, Leader?'

'Why not? I'll be interested to see what he's up to – and whoever he is, he'll never leave here alive.'

The Doctor was marched into central control. It seemed very much the same, though the technicians now wore high-collared military-style white uniforms instead of lab coats, and moved about their duties in a disciplined silence.

The Doctor paused by the digital clock. 'Three hours, twenty-two minutes. You're a lot more advanced here.'

'Come on,' growled Benton, and shoved him along.

The Doctor saw Professor Stahlman and Petra Williams approaching. They wore the same white uniforms as all the others, though theirs were better cut and made of finer material. Otherwise Petra Williams looked much the same, though instead of hanging loose, her long blonde hair was drawn back in a severe bun. This world's Professor Stahlman had no beard. He was wearing dark-tinted glasses – and white gloves.

The Brigade-Leader saluted as Stahlman approached. 'An intruder has been caught inside the complex, Director Stahlman. I thought you might like to question him?'

Stahlman looked incuriously at the Doctor. 'Not really. You know what to do with spies, I take it, Brigade-Leader?'

'He asked to speak to Sir Keith Gold, Director.'

'Indeed? Did you explain to him that this would present certain difficulties?'

The Doctor was getting tired of being discussed as if he wasn't there. 'Difficulties? What difficulties?'

There was faint amusement in Director Stahlman's voice. 'Sir Keith was killed in a motor accident, twenty-four hours ago. Rather unfortunate.'

The Doctor said slowly, 'Sir Keith – dead?'

'I'm afraid so. He was on his way to the Ministry in London.'

'To complain about you, no doubt – about your decision to accelerate the rate of drilling?'

Stahlman said coldly, 'Who is this man, Brigade-Leader?'

'We have not yet discovered his identity, Director. The name he gave us is obviously false.'

'Have you any idea where he comes from?'

'He spoke of coming from some other dimension.'

'I have no time to waste on maniacs, Brigade-Leader.'

'Quite so. My apologies.'

'What about that computer?' said the Doctor suddenly. 'It doesn't appear to be working.' He waved towards the silent computer banks.

'It was sabotaged,' said the Brigade-Leader.

'I'm sure it was. No doubt Director Stahlman could name the culprit. A missing micro-circuit, no doubt?'

Stahlman said, 'Congratulations, Brigade-Leader, you have found your saboteur. It is obvious that this man was responsible for the damage. Take him away.'

51

'Benton!' snapped the Brigade-Leader.

Benton seized the Doctor's arm in a painful grip and marched him off.

Stahlman watched him go thoughtfully. 'Carry on, Doctor Williams,' he said and hurried away.

Greg Sutton appeared, his manner stiff and formal. 'Will you tell the Director that I have no pressure in the coolant pipes?'

'He is aware of that. He ordered the power by-passed to accelerate the drilling.'

'If an emergency develops there will be no safeguards at the drill-head.'

'There will be no emergency.'

Sutton's self-control suddenly gave way. 'Now listen, Petra.'

Petra Williams said icily. 'I am forced to remind you that I am Assistant Director of this project. You will address me in the correct manner.'

Immediately Sutton was humbled. 'I'm sorry, Doctor Williams.'

'Unless you grant me the respect due to my position I shall be forced to report you,' said Petra Williams impassively. She moved away. Yet despite her loyalty to Stahlman, Petra Williams shared some of Sutton's doubts. She passed through the tunnel and went up to Stahlman. As usual he was staring raptly at the drill-head.

Petra consulted the notes on her clip-board. 'All safety factors have now been exceeded, Director.'

Stahlman did not take his eyes from the drill-head. 'We are now very close to penetration. I will not decelerate the drilling at this crucial stage.'

'As you wish, Director.' She moved away.

Once she was out of sight, Stahlman peeled back the glove from the back of his left hand. The knuckles were almost covered in coarse black hair.

The Doctor was standing in front of the Brigade-Leader's desk, Benton at his elbow. There was an armed sentry at the door. The Brigade-Leader was sorting through his papers, pretending that the Doctor wasn't there. It was, thought the

52

Doctor, one of the oldest interrogation techniques in the book.

The Doctor however was getting bored. 'May I ask what is going to happen to me?'

The Brigade-Leader didn't look up. 'You'll be shot – eventually.'

'Without a trial?'

'This is your trial.'

'Nonsense. You can't possibly have the authority.'

'I have full authority, Doctor – under the Defence of the Republic Act of 1943.'

'Republic? What happened to the Royal – '

'Executed – all of them.'

The Doctor sighed. 'Pity. Such a charming family. I knew her great-grandfather in Paris. You know, I remember one evening he said to me, "Doctor," he said, "why don't we go to Maxims and – " '. As he spoke, the Doctor sank into the chair before the desk.

Immediately Benton hauled him to his feet by the scruff of the neck. 'On your feet!'

'I've been standing here for a very long time,' said the Doctor reproachfully.

'You'll be standing a lot longer yet!'

The Doctor fell silent, wondering just what had happened to alter the history of England so drastically. Perhaps the English had lost the Second World War. Or perhaps there had never been a Second World War – not for England, that is. Plenty of people had wanted to make peace with Hitler in 1939, and again in 1940, after Dunkirk. Perhaps in this world they had succeeded. England had kept out of the war, the Americans had stayed neutral, and Hitler was left to rule the Europe he had conquered. Then, sooner or later the Fascists in England would have staged a coup, and set up a Fascist state in the style of their Nazi friends. That was it, decided the Doctor. Not foreign invaders, but Fascism of the home-grown variety.

He shifted his position.

The Brigade-Leader looked up at last, and the Doctor said, 'Tell me, why is this place swarming with your uniformed thugs?'

Benton gave the Doctor a routine thump with his rifle butt.

The Brigade-Leader said, 'You are speaking disrespectfully of the Republican Security Forces – the RSF. We are here because this is a Scientific Labour Camp.'

'Staffed by slave labour, I take it? Well, I warn you, you're all in very grave danger.'

'*We* are in danger?' The Brigade-Leader smiled.

'Before that computer broke down it was transmitting a warning, wasn't it?'

'You are very well informed Doctor.'

'And what about Harry Slocum?'

'How do you know about him?'

'He – changed, didn't he? Went berserk and started killing people?'

The Brigade-Leader paled. News of all these mysterious events had been strictly suppressed. 'You are condemning yourself, Doctor. Only a spy could know so much.'

'Look, I am not a spy, I've seen it all before.'

'Where?' shouted the Brigade-Leader in exasperation.

'In another world,' said the Doctor quietly.

'Very well. I can wait. You will tell me the truth – eventually.'

'You're just wasting time,' said the Doctor wearily.

'We work to an orderly system. Your identity is being checked with Central Records. Once we know who you are the real interrogation can begin.'

'I don't exist in your world!'

'Then you won't feel the bullets when we shoot you,' said the Brigade-Leader calmly.

A buzzer sounded on the desk. He picked up the phone. 'Very well. I'll see you there.'

The Brigade-Leader rose. 'Platoon Under-Leader Benton. The prisoner will remain here.'

The Brigade-Leader hurried away.

He found Section-Leader Shaw waiting for him in central control. She looked badly shaken. 'I've just been on to Central Records, about our prisoner.'

'Well, who is he?'

'There is absolutely no one of his description on their files. The man does not exist.'

'Impossible!'

'They'll keep checking, but they're certain that this man is neither a British National, nor a known agent of any foreign government.'

The Brigade-Leader said slowly, 'Central Records have never been wrong before. Never.'

'Yet the man knows as much about this operation as if he had been here for weeks. It just doesn't make sense.'

They went back to the office.

The Brigade-Leader stared almost indignantly at his prisoner. 'You are giving us a great deal of trouble, Doctor.'

'I'm very glad to hear it!'

'You would make things much easier for yourself if you would tell me the truth.'

The Doctor chuckled. 'Proper little bureaucrat, aren't you? Can't shoot me till you've filled in all the forms, is that it?'

Elizabeth Shaw said, 'Unless you co-operate you will soon be in front of a firing squad. You have very little time.'

'My dear young lady, if that computer out there was still functioning, it would tell us that we all have very little time.'

Petra Williams was talking into an internal phone. 'Number 2 output pipe again? Is the leak bad? I see. Carry on, until further instructions.'

She put down the phone and found Greg Sutton at her elbow.

'Trouble?' he asked.

'Yes.'

'At the drill-head?'

Petra nodded. 'A minor detail.'

'There is no such thing as a minor detail at the drill-head!'

Petra Williams gave him a look. She raised her voice. 'Director?'

Stahlman turned. 'What is it?'

'There's a minor leak in number 2 output pipe.'

'So?'

55

'So we ought to do something about it,' said Sutton. 'We're approaching penetration-zero.'

'Let one of the duty-riggers attend to it.'

'I think you should see for yourself, sir, it could be important.'

'Don't presume to tell me what I should or shouldn't do, Sutton,' snarled Stahlman. He turned away.

'No, Director,' said Sutton woodenly. As Stahlman moved away he muttered, 'Sorry, Director! Three bags full, Director . . .' Greg Sutton had always had a mutinous streak.

Suddenly an alarm screamed out from the drill-head. Instinctively Sutton ran for the tunnel.

In his office the Brigade-Leader reacted too. 'Watch the prisoner,' he ordered and ran from the room. Elizabeth Shaw hurried after him.

Instinctively Benton glanced towards the departing figures. The Doctor's long arm snaked out. Two fingers jabbed Benton under the collar bone, and he crumpled and fell. Stepping over his body, the Doctor ran from the office.

A terrifying shrieking sound was coming from the drill-head.

The Brigade-Leader was speaking into a public address mike set into the wall. His voice boomed out over the wail of the siren. 'Security units alert. All Security units take up positions immediately. No technician will be allowed to leave his post. I say again, no technician will leave his post. All security units alert . . .'

Sutton was herding a group of terrified technicians towards the drill-head. 'Come on, come on, get those heat-suits on.'

The men were climbing into heavy protective disaster-suits.

'Doctor Williams, check the coolant pipes – get me some extra power laid on for the reserve supply.'

As Petra hurried to obey, Sutton drove his emergency team into the tunnel.

Meanwhile, more terrified technicians were running *out*

from the drill-head area. But the Brigade-Leader was ready for them, armed guards behind him. 'Back to your posts!' he shouted. 'Get back or we fire!'

Stahlman's voice bellowed through control. 'We can contain the emergency. All of you, back to your posts!' He glanced round the control area and saw to his astonished rage that the Doctor was working busily at the computer.

Looking round for help, Stahlman saw Benton staggering from the office. 'Benton!' he shouted, and pointed to the Doctor.

Benton nodded, and moved purposefully towards the computer.

The Doctor meanwhile was rooting through a spare-parts locker. 'There must be a spare micro-circuit here somewhere – or even something I could adapt . . .' Something cold and hard touched his head just above the ear. The Doctor turned and found himself gazing straight down the muzzle of a rifle.

On the other end of the rifle was a very angry Benton. 'And what do you think you're doing?'

'Trying to repair your computer for you.'

'Outside,' said Benton curtly. 'I'll have a firing squad ready for you in no time.'

'Don't be an idiot, man. Can't you see how important this is?'

Benton jabbed him hard in the ribs with the rifle barrel. 'On your feet, Doctor.'

Slowly the Doctor rose.

'Now then,' said Benton menacingly. 'Are you coming quietly – or do I shoot you, here and now?'

7

Death Sentence

The Doctor was contemplating these unattractive alternatives when Section-Leader Shaw appeared.

'Just a moment, Under-Leader. What's going on here?'

'Prisoner tried to escape, Leader,' said Benton, woodenly. 'I was about to take him out and shoot him.'

'Not yet, I'll take charge of him.'

Disappointed, Benton stepped back, still keeping the Doctor covered with his rifle.

'Thank you – Section-Leader,' said the Doctor.

'I'm not particularly concerned with saving your skin – only with carrying out the correct procedure.'

The Doctor smiled. 'Well, thank you anyway. Incidentally, I think I may be able to get this computer working again.'

'Leave it alone, Doctor. It's none of your concern.'

'I'd say it was everyone's concern.'

She nodded to Benton. 'Better take him back to the office.'

Benton waved his rifle at the Doctor. 'Come on, you!'

'Just a minute, just a minute,' said the Doctor, and resumed his search through the spare-parts locker.

'I said come on!'

'All right, all right, I'm coming,' said the Doctor, still making no move to obey.

Benton grabbed his arm.

'You might at least let me try. All I have to do is – '

'Come on,' repeated Benton. He tried to drag the Doctor away, but he was astonishingly hard to move.

Suddenly Elizabeth Shaw changed her mind. 'No – wait. Let him try. We've got nothing to lose.'

They watched as the Doctor took a couple of micro circuits, linked them together, removed an access panel and inserted them into the computer. 'There, that ought to hold for a while . . .'

Suddenly the computer came to life. Data began flooding across its screens, and the print-out began spewing out incredibly long rolls of paper.

The Doctor gave a sigh of relief. 'I should say the computer is already aware of the danger and is assessing the immediate problem.' He grabbed the computer print-out strips and began scanning them at amazing speed.

Stahlman came hurrying up. 'What is this man doing here, Section-Leader Shaw?'

'He has repaired the computer, Director.'

'He should not have been allowed near it. He's a dangerous spy. He sabotaged the computer in the first place. Now he's doing it again.'

'I was not sabotaging it,' said the Doctor indignantly. 'I was repairing it, as you can see.'

'The computer is working again, Director,' Elizabeth Shaw pointed out.

'That's right,' said Sutton. 'Shouldn't we see what it's got to say?'

'We are working to my calculations,' said Stahlman.

By now Sutton was openly rebellious. 'Your calculations? And do your calculations tell you how to deal with this emergency?'

'Yes!'

'Well, it doesn't look that way to me.'

'Watch your tongue, Sutton.'

Ignoring him, Sutton turned to the Doctor. 'Can you interpret what the computer is saying?'

'Yes. It's telling us that the combination of pressure and heat is over-powering the velocity of the drill bit.'

'What can we do about it?' asked Petra Williams.

'Disperse the pressure and the heat by creating a reverse vortex at the bottom of the drill shaft.'

Stahlman sneered. 'And how do we do that?'

'Reverse all systems.'

'And bring the project to a standstill?' screamed

Stahlman. 'No!'

'It isn't as crazy as it seems,' insisted Sutton. 'It's been done before, on an oil shaft.'

Stahlman shook his head. 'Out of the question. It could smash the whole system.'

Sutton nodded towards the tunnel to the drill shaft. The screeching was much louder now. 'Sounds to me as if it's smashing itself!'

'That's right,' said the Doctor urgently. 'And what's more, you're wasting time.' He took Sutton's arm. 'Now I suggest you pump the coolant down the output pipes and drag up the debris through the input pipes.'

Sutton looked appealingly at Stahlman. 'Well, Director?'

Stahlman hesitated a moment longer. The hideous sounds from the drill shaft made up his mind for him. He raised his voice. 'Reverse all systems. Bypass number 2 output pipe.'

Under the watchful eyes of the Brigade-Leader's men, the technicians hurried to their tasks.

Stahlman turned to the Brigade-Leader. 'Now, will you get that man out of my control room!'

'Take him away, Benton.'

'You might let me see if the idea works. Of all the ungrateful nitwits!' Still protesting, the Doctor was bustled away.

Back in the Brigade-Leader's office, the Doctor stood listening for any change in the shrieking sound coming from the drill-head.

Elizabeth Shaw looked curiously at him. 'You seem to know a great deal about this project.'

'Enough.'

'You really are a scientist.'

'Of sorts.'

'Where did you come from, Doctor?'

'I've already told you that. I come from a parallel space/time continuum – a sort of twin world to this.'

'If you'd only tell us the truth, Doctor, there might be some hope for you.'

'Your counterpart in that other world knows I am not in the habit of telling lies.'

60

'This other woman – the one that looks like me – '

'It isn't that she looks like you,' interrupted the Doctor, 'she is you. I wish I could make you understand that.'

'What does she do?'

'She's a scientist.'

'And I'm a security officer.'

'Yes,' said the Doctor thoughtfully. 'But tell me, did you ever want to be a scientist?' He studied her face. 'Yes, I can see you did.'

'I took a doctorate in science,' she said slowly. 'What has that got to do with this ridiculous story of yours?'

'Just that your mind-processes run on similar lines to hers – the other Liz. Don't you find that significant?'

'Not particularly.'

'Please, Liz, try to think,' urged the Doctor. 'Whatever they've taught you in this twisted world, you've still got a mind of your own. Use it – while you've still got time!'

The shrieking from the drill-head was beginning to fade. Greg Sutton looked at Petra Williams. 'It's working. Who was that funny-looking bloke anyway?'

She shrugged. 'They say he's a saboteur.'

'So how come he saves all our necks?'

'He was probably just trying to save his own. Hadn't you better get number 2 output pipe fixed?'

'It'll mean cutting down the drill to minimum revs.'

'The Director won't like that.'

'He'll have to lump it,' said Sutton bluntly. 'There's no alternative.'

Petra Williams looked sadly at him. 'If only you could curb this rebellious streak, Sutton, you might have a great future as a servant of the State.'

'Thanks a lot,' said Sutton ironically. 'And be a nice well-behaved little zombie like the rest of you? No thanks.'

'You survive only because your technical skills have a certain value, Sutton. Once this project is over – '

'Greg Sutton is for the high jump? A little accident in the cells – shot while trying to escape?'

'These things happen.'

He looked hard at her. 'And would you care?'

61

Petra Williams hesitated, then turned away. 'I should regret the waste, that's all.'

Elizabeth Shaw said, 'Yes, I see. Thank you.' She put down the phone. 'The emergency is over.'

'I'm glad to hear it,' said the Doctor cheerfully.

'It seems your idea worked.'

'Maybe you could give me a medal – posthumously of course.'

'You find the idea of death amusing, Doctor?'

'Not particularly. Do you?'

Her voice was almost pleading. 'If you told me the true facts about yourself I might be able to help you.'

'My dear Liz, I am trying to help you. You just said the emergency was over. Well, it isn't. As long as you people go on drilling, you're all rushing into terrible danger.'

In the drill-head area Greg Sutton stood supervising a gang of riggers as they repaired the broken output pipe.

Stahlman stood by impatiently. 'How long, Sutton? How long?'

'Almost finished.'

'Good. Then we shall continue with the drilling.'

'At reduced revs?'

Stahlman shook his head. 'It is my intention to accelerate again as soon as possible.'

'I don't advise it, Director.'

'I don't need anyone's advice.'

'Not even that prisoner's?'

'I would have reached the same conclusions.'

'You might have reached them a bit too late.'

'You know, Sutton, I sometimes wonder why I tolerate your insolence.'

Greg Sutton smiled. 'Because on a project like this, you need more than a good party member – you need a good engineer.'

Stahlman said grimly, 'Perhaps. But remember, Sutton, although you are useful, you are not indispensable.'

'This seems to be my day for getting warnings.'

'You have a bad record, Sutton,' warned Stahlman. 'A

long history of insubordination. It would be very easy to have you disposed of. Remember that.' Stahlman turned abruptly away and headed off down the tunnel.

Half-way down he paused, hands over his ears. For a moment it seemed as if the terrible screeching that had been coming from the drill-shaft was sounding inside his head.

The Doctor was sitting in the chair before the Brigade-Leader's desk. Benton stood behind him, pulling his head back at a painful angle. The powerful lamp on the desk had been swivelled round so that it shone directly into the Doctor's face. His interrogation had begun.

They hadn't got to the real rough stuff, not yet. One or two thumps from Benton, just to soften him up a little. Now they were relying on the tried and true methods – the cramped, uncomfortable position, the light blazing into the face so that he could see nothing of the Brigade-Leader and Section-Leader Shaw standing behind it; and above all, the questions, endlessly repeated, hammering into the brain.

'Name?' shouted Section-Leader Shaw.

'Who sent you?' demanded the Brigade-Leader.

One after the other they rapped out their questions.

'Did you come to commit sabotage?'

'Name?'

'What organisation do you belong to?'

'When did you first become a traitor?'

'How did you get into the complex?'

'Who helped you?' demanded the Brigade-Leader. 'Was it Sutton?'

'Name?' insisted Liz. 'Tell us your name!'

'Answer!'

'You're wasting your time, you know,' said the Doctor. 'I can stand a great deal of this childishness.'

'This is only the beginning,' warned the Brigade-Leader.

'There are other methods,' threatened Section-Leader Shaw.

'I'm sure there are,' said the Doctor wearily. 'They won't do you any good.'

'You'll talk eventually,' said the Brigade-Leader confidently. 'Everybody talks.'

'You can't make me give you information that doesn't exist.'

'The information does exist, Doctor – and you will give it to us,' bellowed the Brigade-Leader.

'Name?' demanded Section-Leader Shaw remorselessly.

'Who sent you here?' repeated the Brigade-Leader.

The unending round of questions began again.

'Which enemy power do you work for?'

'Who are your associates?'

'How did you get here?'

'I came alone, and by accident.' The Doctor's voice was a little weaker now. 'The TARDIS slipped me sideways . . .'

Elizabeth Shaw looked at the Brigade-Leader. 'Perhaps we should proceed to stage two interrogation? He's just babbling.'

The Brigade-Leader considered. 'No. He's a tough one. He might die before he talked.'

'Perhaps we'd better let him get his strength back . . .'

Suddenly the room began to vibrate. The noise of the drill had been almost inaudible at minimum revs, but now it had started up again louder and shriller than before.

The Doctor leaped to his feet. 'It's Stahlman – he's accelerated the drilling!'

At a nod from the Brigade-Leader, Benton grabbed the Doctor's shoulders and slammed him back into the chair. His head was pulled back, the light trained on his face.

'All right,' said the Brigade-Leader. 'We'll begin again, shall we?'

'Name?'

'Who sent you here?'

'Why did you come here?'

The door was flung open, and Stahlman came into the room. 'What progress have you made?'

The Brigade-Leader said stiffly. 'As you can see, Director, the prisoner is being interrogated. We are proceeding according to plan.'

Wrenching his head away from Benton's hands, the Doctor struggled to sit upright. 'I see you are wearing gloves, Director. May we know why?'

'Brigade-Leader – you are allowing the prisoner to be impertinent.'

'Go on,' said the Doctor. 'Ask him to take them off. I think you'll find it very interesting.'

Suddenly Stahlman laughed. 'Why not? They say madmen should be humoured.' He peeled off his left glove to reveal a neatly bandaged hand.

'Why the bandages?' challenged the Doctor.

Stahlman shrugged. 'I scorched my hand on a section of the drill-head.'

'Oh no,' said the Doctor softly. 'A drop of that green substance from the output pipe touched you, didn't it? Just a little, but enough to infect you – like all those others.' There was something very convincing in the Doctor's voice.

The Brigade-Leader looked at the Director's face, twisted with rage, and suddenly felt very uncomfortable.

'All right, we've wasted enough time,' he said abruptly. 'Take him away, Benton, down to the security cells.'

The Doctor was heaved to his feet.

'Stahlman, you've got to listen. You're very ill. You've been infected. I think this terrible compulsion to reach penetration-zero is part of that sickness.'

'Take him away,' screamed Stahlman.

The Doctor was dragged out.

The Brigade-Leader snapped, 'Section-Leader Shaw, you will supervise the transfer of the prisoner to the security block.'

'At once, Brigade-Leader.' She followed the Doctor and Benton from the room.

The Brigade-Leader studied Stahlman thoughtfully. 'You take a great interest in this prisoner, Director?'

'The security of this project – '

' – is my responsibility,' completed the Brigadier.

'Yet you have allowed this man to enter the complex and roam about apparently at will.'

'The man was caught, Director. And caught quickly. He is no longer a danger to us. But the information he can give us, about the people who sent him, how and why he came here – that information is vital.'

'Then I suggest you make the Doctor talk. But do it quickly. Before this day is over, I want him liquidated – and that, Brigade-Leader, is an order!'

8

Countdown to Doom

Raising their voices to counter the increased sound from the drill-head, Petra Williams and Greg Sutton were arguing as usual.

'We should have checked out the whole system from top to bottom while we still had the drill at minimum revs,' Greg Sutton was saying.

Petra shook her head. 'The Director wouldn't permit the delay. He knows what he's doing.'

'You make a little tin god of Stahlman, don't you? I think he's a nut.'

'That kind of talk is very dangerous.'

'He's a nut I tell you. He's obsessed.' Sutton looked hard at her. 'Well, are you going to report me? Get me a week in the punishment cells?'

Petra was silent.

Greg Sutton smiled. 'Hey, things are looking up,' he said teasingly. 'A few days ago you'd have turned me in without a second thought!'

It was the Doctor who was in the cells, a row of cages along a narrow passage, separated only by their bars. It was like being in a zoo.

The cage next to the Doctor's was occupied by a still form under a rough blanket. Whoever he was, the man was apparently fast asleep.

As Benton unlocked the door of his future cell, the Doctor was saying, 'I'll have you know your counterpart on the other Earth is a nice sociable sort of fellow, Sergeant.'

'My rank is Platoon Under-Leader,' said Benton stolidly.

'Bit of a mouthful, isn't it?'

'Your trouble is, you talk too much.'

The Doctor nodded towards the prisoner in the next cell. 'What did he do? Park in a restricted zone?'

'Stop asking stupid questions.'

The Doctor glanced at the motionless huddled shape. 'Well, at least he seems to be sleeping peacefully.'

'Tranquilliser dart,' said Benton curtly. 'They don't give us much trouble after that. We should have done the same to you. Now, get in.' He thrust the Doctor inside the cell, slammed and locked the door, and turned and went away.

'Any chance of some food?' called the Doctor plaintively. 'Cup of tea? Glass of water, then?'

To his surprise Benton reappeared, this time with Section-Leader Shaw and another sentry.

'Visiting time already, is it?' said the Doctor cheerfully.

'Your interrogation isn't over yet.'

'Oh, yes it is,' said the Doctor, and stretched out on the bunk.

'Get on your feet when the Section-Leader's talking to you!' shouted Benton.

'Oh, go away and give me some peace.'

'When I say get on your feet, prisoner, I mean get on your feet!'

'All right,' grumbled the Doctor. 'Anything for a quiet life!' He got up and leaned against the bars.

'Now,' said Section-Leader Shaw relentlessly. 'We'll start again. Who sent you? How did you get into the complex?'

'I am sick and tired of being badgered with all these questions!'

'The questions will go on until you answer them!'

'I have answered them – more times than I care to think about!'

'You have told us nothing.'

'I have told you the truth – it's not my fault if your minds are too narrow to accept it.'

Benton looked longingly at the Doctor. 'Just let me have a few minutes with him, Leader.'

'No,' she snapped. 'Wait outside – both of you.'

Benton and the sentry moved away.

She turned to the Doctor. 'Now perhaps we can talk sensibly.'

'Trying a change of tactics?'

'If you like.'

'First the bullying, then the charm,' said the Doctor cynically. 'Secret police tactic number two!'

'Believe me, Doctor, I really am trying to help you.'

'Even though you think I'm a spy?'

She shook her head. 'No. You're far too conspicuous to be a spy. I think you come from one of those crackpot free speech groups. You're making some sort of demonstration.'

'Oh no!' groaned the Doctor.

She leaned forward. 'If you'll make a full confession, I may be able to convince them you're just a harmless lunatic. You'll get off with a few years in a labour camp.'

The Doctor gripped the bars of his cell. 'I am not mad. I am not a spy and I am certainly not a political demonstrator. You just won't listen, will you?'

'I can see I've been wasting my time,' said Elizabeth Shaw coldly. 'I'll leave it to the Brigade-Leader. He'll get the truth out of you.'

'Your counterpart had a great deal of intelligence, Liz,' said the Doctor wearily. 'I wish I could say the same for you.'

She moved away.

The Doctor sat down on his bunk. He glanced across at the sleeping prisoner in the next cell. 'Hullo, old chap! How are you doing? Been down here long?' Silence. The Doctor tried again. 'Read any good police records lately?'

There was no reply.

The Doctor stretched out on his bunk. 'The friendliness of this establishment overwhelms me.'

The prisoner opposite muttered and stirred.

The Doctor had his back turned. He didn't see the hand that emerged from beneath the blanket.

It was not so much a hand as a claw, covered with thick, coarse hair.

Back in the world that the Doctor had so suddenly and strangely left, the Brigadier and Liz Shaw – the familiar friendly Brigadier and Liz – were gazing sadly around the Doctor's empty hut.

'I'm sorry, Miss Shaw,' said the Brigadier. 'My men have searched the entire complex – thoroughly. There's just no sign of the Doctor.'

Liz nodded. 'I didn't really think there would be.'

'Maybe that wretched machine of his just dumped him a few miles away?' suggested the Brigadier hopefully.

'I don't think it's as simple as that, Brigadier. He's somewhere else. Lost somewhere in space and time.'

'Well, wherever he is – or whenever he is, the Doctor can look after himself,' said the Brigadier with determined cheerfulness.

Liz gave him a reproachful look. 'Even the Doctor's not indestructible, you know.'

Looking somewhat incongruous in black jacket and striped trousers, Homburg hat and rolled umbrella, Sir Keith Gold made his way across the control room to Professor Stahlman.

'I wonder if you could spare me a moment, Professor?'

Stahlman looked up from his clip-board. 'Run out of paperwork?' he asked rudely. 'Well?'

'Are there any problems with the accelerated drilling?'

'None at all. I didn't expect any.'

'But no doubt you will be taking extra precautions as we approach penetration-zero?'

'I shall do what I think best. Now, what is it you want?'

'I have a car waiting to take me up to London for an appointment with the Minister.'

'Have a pleasant journey.'

Sir Keith braced himself. 'Unless you can give me certain assurances, I shall have to inform the Minister of the full extent of my anxieties regarding this project.'

'Assurances? What assurances?'

'We must slow down the drilling rate. We need improved safety precautions. We need a fail-safe mechanism so that we can close down completely if necessary.'

Stahlman turned on him in a rage. 'If you'd had your way, we would never have started this project. Now you want me to proceed at a snail's pace, like a cautious old woman. Well, I conceived this project. I fought for Government backing, and I shall carry it through to success in spite of all you can do to stop me. You have consistently obstructed my work and I do not intend to tolerate your interference any longer. You can tell the Minister what you like, Sir Keith. He, at least, is aware of the importance of my work.'

Liz and the Brigadier entered the control area in time to hear the last of this diatribe.

Sir Keith came over to them. He managed a rueful smile.

'He doesn't get any better does he?' said the Brigadier sympathetically.

'He's impossible.'

'Do you think the Minister will listen?' asked Liz.

'Well, he is an old friend of mine – but I'm afraid Stahlman has dazzled him with promises of limitless free power.'

'Will you be back in time for penetration-zero?'

'Yes, indeed, though I can't say I'm looking forward to it. I know it sounds ridiculous, but I feel there's something ominous about this entire project. I think your friend the Doctor felt it too . . . By the way, where did he go to?'

'We're not quite sure,' said the Brigadier diplomatically.

Sir Keith sighed. 'Well, he's better off out of it, wherever he is . . .'

In the parallel world, the Doctor woke up. Something had awakened him. Then he realised. An eerie screeching and moaning was coming from the next cell. The Doctor sat up.

The figure under the blanket was twisting and thrashing about as if in the throes of some kind of fit.

The Doctor raised his voice. 'Sentry! Sentry, where are you? Sentry!'

The door was flung open and a sleepy, bad-tempered soldier clattered down the corridor. 'What's all the row about?'

The Doctor pointed to the next cell. 'That man is sick. He needs medical attention.'

The sentry peered through the bars at the writhing figure in the cell. 'Hey, you. If you don't shut up, I'll shut you up!'

There was no reply. Only the hideous moaning and snarling. The sentry produced a key, opened the cell door and went inside. 'All right, you,' he snarled. He ripped the blanket from the writhing form – and stepped back, gaping in horror. The figure under the blanket was no longer human; the face was sprouting patches of hair, and the teeth were yellow fangs.

It must be one of the infected technicians, the Doctor realised. Bromley, was it? In this world he had been captured and tranquillised in the early stages of the infection. But the recessive mutation had continued while he was unconscious and now it was almost complete.

The Doctor looked on horrified and powerless as the red-eyed terrifying figure leaped on the sentry. Roaring and snarling, the creature hurled the sentry to the ground, throttling the life out of him with powerful claws. Letting the body fall, the mutant straightened up – and saw the Doctor. It advanced towards him. The Doctor backed away, thankful for the protection of the bars between the cells.

The monster gripped two of the bars in its powerful claws and began bending them apart as if they were made of rubber. Horrified, the Doctor saw the gap grow larger, larger . . . As soon as it was big enough the creature started to squeeze through into the Doctor's cell.

There were only two pieces of furniture in the cell, the stool and the bed, and the Doctor used them both. As the monster sprang, he snatched up the wooden stool and smashed it down over its head. The creature staggered back. It was dazed and hurt, but by no means out of action. It stood roaring, swinging its head to and fro. Then it charged again.

The Doctor was ready. He heaved up the heavy wooden bed, mattress and all, and smashed it down on the mutant, bearing it to the ground. As the monster struggled wildly to free itself, the Doctor leaped over the bed, slipped through the gap into the next cell, jumped over the dead body of the sentry and went through the now-open door of the cell and out into the corridor.

The key to the cell was still in the lock. The Doctor locked the cell behind him and ran from the building.

Throwing off mattress and bed, the monster staggered to its feet. It looked around, roaring with rage. Then it shambled to the door of the Doctor's cell and began wrenching it from its hinges. Minutes later it was lurching down the corridor in pursuit of the Doctor.

A few minutes later, Platoon Under-Leader Benton came by the cells on a routine check – and discovered that everything was very far from well.

He took in the dead sentry, the wrecked cells, the widened bars, the cell door hanging off its hinges, and above all, the absence of the Doctor.

With a shout of alarm, he turned and ran from the cell.

The Doctor ran out of the cell-block and found himself outside one of a number of low concrete buildings. There was some kind of van standing outside the nearest, and he ran towards it.

He was heading for the driving seat when he heard someone coming round the corner of the building. Instinctively, the Doctor dived for the only cover available – the back of the van. He pulled open the rear doors and jumped inside, closing the doors behind him.

The approaching someone got into the front of the van and drove away.

As they jolted along, the Doctor realised he had landed on something relatively soft. Investigating, he discovered that it was a pile of disaster suits, heavy, all-concealing garments made from some kind of heavy canvas impregnated with flame-proof protective chemicals. The suits had built-in boots, gauntlets, and a helmet with a smoked-glass visor. All in all, the Doctor decided they formed as effective a disguise as he was likely to find. Laboriously, be began struggling into one of the suits. As he did so, he became aware that they were driving towards some kind of activity. He heard hooting sirens, marching feet, and shouted orders . . .

It sounded as if something very significant was about to happen.

In central control, all was bustle and excitement. They were within minutes of penetration-zero.

The technicians were being herded to their positions by

the Brigade-Leader's men.

Greg Sutton and Assistant Director Petra Williams stood watching these final preparations.

Sutton was openly nervous. 'Everything all right?'

'All systems have been checked and are functional,' said Petra coolly.

'We'd better keep our fingers crossed.'

'We depend on science, Mr Sutton, not superstition.'

'We could do with some plain old-fashioned luck as well!' Sutton looked around. 'Where's the Director?'

'He'll be here.'

'I wish I wasn't,' said Sutton fervently. 'Something's wrong. Something's just not adding up.'

'What can go wrong?'

He shrugged. 'Perhaps we should try asking the computer.'

The truck jolted to a halt and the door was flung open. The Doctor saw that he was surrounded by soldiers. For a moment he thought everything was lost. Then he noticed the foremost soldier looking expectantly at him. The Doctor grabbed a disaster suit and handed it out. It was obviously the right thing to do.

The Doctor passed out disaster suits to the soldiers and technicians milling around the truck until the truck was empty. Then he jumped out and joined the line of already-suited figures filing into central control.

As he went inside a voice boomed, '*Zero minus three minutes zero seconds. Condition Red 2 now commencing.*'

The Doctor slipped away from the line, walked over to the computer and studied the latest print-outs. It was even worse than he had feared.

The countdown continued. '*Zero minus two minutes ten seconds. Disaster crew to action stations.*'

He heard the Brigade-Leader's voice close by. 'You there, get back to your post!'

The countdown voice said, '*Zero minus one minute forty seconds. Technical personnel to final stations.*'

The Doctor looked up and saw the Brigade-Leader standing over him, revolver in hand. 'You there! Didn't you hear what I said?'

'*Zero minus one minute ten seconds. All systems checked for final countdown.*'

Horrified, the Doctor finished reading the last print-out.

'*Zero minus one minute zero seconds. Countdown commences now!*'

'You there – for the last time!' shouted the Brigade-Leader 'Come here.'

'*Zero minus fifty seconds. Stand by.*'

The Doctor whipped off his helmet. 'You must stop this countdown before it's too late. Do you hear me? You must stop it!'

Stahlman saw what was happening and came running across. He was almost beserk with rage at the idea of any interruption. 'Brigade-Leader shoot this man – immediately.'

'You can't do that,' protested Sutton. 'It's just murder!'

The Doctor shouted, 'If you break through the Earth's crust now you'll release forces you never dreamed could exist!'

'*Zero minus twenty seconds. Countdown moves to final phase.*'

By now the roaring from the drill-head had reached a higher, shattering level and once more it had a kind of screeching quality.

'Listen to that,' shouted the Doctor. 'It's the sound of this planet screaming out its rage. You must stop drilling.'

The noise was deafening, and they were all shouting now.

Stahlman screamed, 'Brigade-Leader, I ordered you to shoot that man!'

The Brigade-Leader levelled his revolver at the Doctor's head. It was quite obvious that he was going to obey Stahlman's order.

Greg Sutton jumped him, bearing him to the ground. 'Go on, Doctor,' he yelled. 'Run for it!'

The revolver was jarred from the Brigade-Leader's hand and the two men rolled over, struggling furiously.

'*Zero minus twenty seconds – countdown will proceed by seconds.*'

The Doctor turned to run – and found Benton blocking his escape.

Stahlman snatched up the revolver, levelling it at the Doctor's head. He paused, almost as if prolonging the pleasure of the moment.

The countdown voice said, '*Zero minus ten . . . nine . . . eight . . . seven . . . six . . . five . . . four . . . three . . . two . . . one . . .*'

9

Penetration-Zero

'Zero!' boomed the countdown voice. *'We have penetration-zero.'*

Somewhere deep inside the drill-head there was a colossal explosion. The control room shuddered so violently that most of those inside were thrown off their feet, including Stahlman himself. For a moment there was total confusion. The air was filled with the screams of terrified technicians, the wailing of alarm systems and, underneath everything, the deep menacing roar that came from the drill-head.

Stahlman had lost the revolver in his fall, but he made no attempt to look for it. His desire to kill the Doctor was as nothing beside his obsessive concern for his project. 'Get back!' he screamed at the fleeing technicians. 'Get back to your posts!'

It was the Brigade-Leader who recovered the revolver. He advanced determinedly on Sutton as if determined to avenge the assault on his dignity.

Sutton himself just climbed to his feet and was immediately grabbed by a couple of the Brigade-Leader's men. Angrily he shook them off. 'Do you mind? I've got a job to do here!' He ran to a wall-locker, pulled out a spare disaster-suit, and began climbing into it.

'All right, never mind him for now,' ordered the Brigade-Leader. 'Cover all the doors – and get those technicians back to their posts!'

Petra Williams hurried over to Stahlman, who was studying one of the power consoles. 'Are you all right, Director?'

'Yes, yes,' he said impatiently. 'Check the other control stations.'

After being very much the centre of attention, the Doctor

75

suddenly found himself ignored. He made his way over to Sutton, who was zipping up his disaster-suit.

The Doctor pointed towards the tunnel. 'You're not thinking of going in there, are you?' he shouted.

'Don't worry! I've never seen a drill bore I couldn't cap.'

'There's never been a bore like this one!'

'First thing to do is have a look in there and get the coolant reserve flowing.'

Stahlman moved past them, obviously heading for the drill-head.

Sutton reached out and grabbed his arm. 'If you're going in there, Director, you'd better put one of these suits on.'

Stahlman glared wildly at him, snatched his arm free and ran into the tunnel.

'Somehow I don't think he feels the heat as much as we do,' said the Doctor drily.

They headed for the tunnel.

Section-Leader Shaw saw them from the other side of central control. She turned to Petra Williams, who was checking readings on a nearby console. 'Can't they control the emergency from here?'

Petra shook her head. 'They'll have to go into the actual drill-head for that.'

The Doctor and Sutton paused at the threshold of the tunnel. There was a fiery glow at the far end. It felt rather like jumping into a furnace.

The Doctor adjusted his helmet. 'Well, here goes!'

They plunged into the tunnel, staggered along it fighting the overpowering heat, and emerged into the drill-head area. The Doctor's first thought was that it really was an inferno. The heat was so great that the air shimmered in front of them. The drill-shaft tube was buckled and smoke was pouring out – smoke and flame and an ooze of glowing green slime. The bodies of collapsed technicians were strewn everywhere, some obviously dead, others overcome by the heat or knocked out by the blast of the explosion.

The Doctor began dragging a technician away from the edge of the drill-head, while Sutton went to wrestle with the massive wheel that controlled the reserve coolant supply. It had jammed with the heat. He began heaving with all his strength. It wouldn't budge.

The Doctor looked up to see how Sutton was getting on – just in time to see Stahlman loom up behind him and strike him down with a length of piping. Grabbing Sutton's unconscious body, Stahlman began dragging him towards the drill-head. The Doctor ran up to them, seized Stahlman and pulled him away. Dropping the semi-conscious Sutton, Stahlman turned, and attacked the Doctor with savage ferocity and inhuman strength.

The strange force that had taken over Stahlman made him immune to the Doctor's Venusian aikido, and he even withstood the fearsome Martian karate. Blows, kicks and throws had no effect. Ignoring all the Doctor's efforts to defend himself, Stahlman grabbed him by the throat and began to throttle him, forcing him to his knees.

Suddenly, in a strange reversal of the incident of a few moments ago, Greg Sutton appeared behind Stahlman, with Stahlman's abandoned length of piping in his hands, and clubbed Stahlman down with all his strength. Letting go of the Doctor, Stahlman fell groaning to his knees.

The Doctor and Sutton, both equally groggy, helped each other towards the relative safety of the tunnel. As they emerged into central control, Sutton gasped. 'What was all that about? What the blazes hit me?'

'A piece of piping,' said the Doctor. 'Held by Stahlman.'

'Stahlman hit me?'

Petra came running up. 'Is the Director still in there?'

'He is indeed,' said the Doctor.

'Why didn't he come out with you?'

'I think he likes it in there!'

Sutton rubbed his aching head. 'The main coolant valve's seized up. I can't flood the drill-head area!'

'We've got to get the Professor out of there,' cried Petra.

'Not to mention those technicians,' said the Doctor. 'Mr Sutton?'

A couple of technicians in disaster suits were waiting for orders, and Sutton beckoned them over. 'All right, you two, with me. Come on, Doc, we'll have another go.'

Suddenly there was a grinding, metallic rumble as a heavy metal shield descended, closing off the end of the tunnel.

'What the heck's going on?' shouted Sutton.

Petra ran to a control panel. 'They've closed off the heat shield – from the inside, locked it down on manual!'

Sutton shook his head. 'But that's crazy . . .'

More glowing green slime was oozing from the edge of the drill-head. Stahlman moved about the area, scooping up handfuls of the slime and rubbing it into the face of the unconscious technicians.

He had torn off his gloves, and the claw-like hands were covered with coarse black hair . . .

The Doctor went over to the computer and studied the latest print-out. The others joined him.

'What does it say?' asked Petra.

'Very little, I'm afraid. Tell me, Mr Sutton, how thick are these walls?'

'Thick enough. Ferrous concrete, steel plating, asbestos panelling, the lot. They'd stand up to an atomic blast.'

'Compared to the forces you people have unleashed,' said the Doctor witheringly, 'an atomic blast would be like a summer breeze!'

By now most of the surrounding countryside was aware that some disaster had struck the project. A thick plume of black smoke was pouring out of the centre of the complex, and the sky around was beginning to take on a pinkish glow. From all over the country, reports of earth-tremors were flooding in. In some places strange cracks and fissures had appeared in the earth – some of them were giving off thick clouds of smoke . . .

Brigade-Leader Lethbridge Stewart marched back into central control looking both angry and flustered. Section-Leader Shaw was with him.

'Well, Brigade-Leader,' said the Doctor ironically. 'What's happening in the outside world?'

'The technicians and staff have already cleared out, and most of my security guards seem to have gone with them.'

Sutton said, 'Maybe they're the sensible ones.'

78

'They'll be no better off,' said the Doctor sombrely. 'Wherever they go.'

The others looked at him, not taking in the full meaning of his words.

Petra came over from the computer. 'Well, that's it. The computer has finally packed up.'

The Doctor said, 'The heat must have fused the main circuits. I'll go and have a look.' He wandered off.

'Any news from London, Brigade-Leader?' asked Petra Williams.

'Massive seismic disturbances all over the country. Earth tremors registered in the Midlands and as far north as Leeds.'

'And what are the authorities doing?' demanded Sutton.

Section-Leader Shaw said, 'They've ordered the immediate evacuation of the entire area. The Brigade-Leader is to assume executive control of this project.'

'Any more good news?'

'No. After that the line went dead.'

Sutton said bitterly, 'So, they're abandoning us. They're not even going to try to seal that shaft.'

'They believe that the emergency will eventually pass over,' said Elizabeth Shaw loyally.

Sutton nodded towards the Doctor. 'He doesn't seem to think so.'

'Who cares what he thinks?' snapped the Brigade-Leader.

'I do! He talks a lot of sense.' Sutton crossed to the Doctor. 'Listen, there must be some way we can seal off that shaft. Suppose they evacuated us, blew up the whole area?'

The Doctor shook his head. 'Too late, Mr Sutton. You have released the energies at the Earth's core.' A menacing rumble from the drill-head seemed to underline his words.

'But we must cap the bore somehow.'

'No substance on this Earth is strong enough to withstand the pressure.'

Sutton stared at him, still unable to take in the full extent of the catastrophe. To him this was just another drilling emergency, bigger than most, but still solvable – somehow. 'So, what's going to happen?'

'Yes, Doctor,' said the Brigade-Leader. 'What is going to happen?'

The Doctor hesitated, then decided to tell the truth. 'The heat and the pressure will build up till the Earth dissolves into a fury of expanding gases – just as it was millions of years ago.'

There was a stunned silence.

Elizabeth Shaw said quietly. 'How long have we got?'

'Maybe a few weeks. Maybe only a few days.'

'Then – Doomsday?' said Sutton bitterly. 'And we just sit back and wait for it – '

A savage roar interrupted his words. Everyone turned. A terrifying figure stood swaying in the doorway. It wore the tattered remnants of a technician's uniform, but the face and the eyes were those of a savage beast. It was the Doctor's former cell-companion, though now the recessive mutation had progressed a good deal further.

'Don't go near him,' warned the Doctor. 'He's probably more interested in reaching the heat from the drill-head than he is in us.'

The creature shambled towards the sealed tunnel, its path bringing it close to the little group.

For a moment it looked as if it would pass them by – but as the creature shambled closer, the Brigade-Leader panicked. Snatching out his revolver, he opened fire, pumping all six bullets into the creature's body. To his horror it did not die. Instead it swung round roaring, and lurched towards him.

Ironically, it was the Doctor who saved the Brigade-Leader's life. Snatching up a fire-extinguisher he enveloped the monster in a freezing cloud of CO_2 gas.

It staggered and fell.

The Doctor moved cautiously nearer, examining the body. 'It seems to be dead this time.'

The Brigade-Leader was reloading his revolver. 'Scarcely surprising.'

'Not because of your bullets – or not entirely. The gas from the fire-extinguisher. They can't stand cold, you see.'

Sutton looked down at the twisted body and shuddered. 'Well, that's enough for me. No sense in hanging on round here.'

The Brigadier turned threateningly on him. 'I warn you, Sutton, if you're thinking of leaving – '

'Evacuating is the word, Brigade-Leader. If I've got a little time left I want to spend it well away from here.'

'We were ordered to remain,' said the Brigade-Leader 'And that is exactly what we are going to do. You still have a job to do here Sutton.'

'You just don't listen, do you? You heard what the Doctor said. It's all over. Nothing we can do, isn't that right, Doc?'

'I'm afraid so.'

'Exactly,' said Sutton. 'Well, I'm off. Coming Petra?'

Petra Williams hesitated.

The Brigade-Leader said, 'You will both stay here and do your duty.'

Sutton laughed. 'Still loyal to the glorious republic. I'd like to know what your precious dictator can do for you now.'

'I will not listen to treason!' shouted the Brigade-Leader.

'Gentlemen, please,' said the Doctor wearily. 'There's no sense in arguing. Save your energy.'

Platoon Under-Leader Benton appeared. 'I've managed to round up a few of the men, Leader.'

'Excellent. Post them outside, cover all exits. No one leaves this building without my authority, Benton. No one.'

'Understood, Leader.' Benton saluted.

The Brigade-Leader returned the salute, and Benton marched away.

Sutton laughed hollowly. 'Marvellous, isn't it? The world's going up in flames, and they're still playing soldiers.'

Platoon Under-Leader Benton posted his men at strategic points about the building. They moved along uneasily, disturbed by the uncanny heat, the reddish glow in the sky, and the dull rumblings from the drill-head.

Numbly they obeyed Benton's commands, hoping desperately that, somehow, obeying orders, not thinking, would save them.

Petra Williams was working on the computer, trying to ignore Greg Sutton's arguments that she was wasting her time. In her heart she knew that he was probably right, but it was better to be doing something.

Suddenly her defences seemed to crumble. 'Greg, I'm frightened,' she sobbed. 'What are we going to do?'

Sutton put an arm round her shoulders. 'I'm going to get out of here – and I could do with some help. Are you going to go on being a good little zombie? Or are you going to join the rebels?'

In the Brigade-Leader's office, an official voice was blaring from the radio. 'In London the Minister of Energy and Resources has made a statement about the drilling project in East Manchester. The entire operation has now been cancelled, and the area is being evacuated . . .'

There was more, but static made it almost inaudible. Section-Leader Shaw switched off the radio. 'Perhaps we ought to evacuate, Brigade-Leader?'

'I shall decide that.'

'But if there's nothing we can do . . .'

'You could help to save a world,' said the Doctor unexpectedly.

'You said we'd passed the point of no return.'

'Not this world, Elizabeth. The other one. It exists, you know. It's as real as the one you know yourself.'

'And we're all somehow duplicated there?'

'You, Lethbridge-Stewart here, Sutton, Miss Williams, Stahlman, you Liz. You could save those other selves.'

'How?'

'With the help of the TARDIS.'

'That odd-looking contraption we found in the hut?'

'That's right.'

'Could it take you back?'

'Perhaps. If I could get power from your nuclear reactor.'

'But if this other world is parallel to us, surely they'll be in exactly the same situation?'

'Not necessarily. Work on their project isn't so advanced. I might be able to stop them before they penetrate the Earth's crust.'

The Brigade-Leader had been listening to this

conversation with surprising interest. Suddenly he got to his feet. 'Come along, Doctor. I think we'll take another look at this wonderful machine of yours.'

10

The Monsters

The Brigade-Leader stared at the TARDIS console in deep disgust. 'You expect me to believe you came here in this? It isn't a vehicle at all.'

'It's a very important part of one. In the world I come from, I removed this console to make some trial runs.' The Doctor patted the console affectionately. He flicked a couple of switches and the TARDIS began vibrating slightly, giving off a faint hum of power.

The Brigade-Leader jumped back. 'What's happening? You said you needed a power source to make this thing work!'

'There's a minimal amount of power left in the storage unit,' explained the Doctor. 'Just enough for me to check the circuits.'

'Well, I think we've seen enough of this nonsense. We shall return to central control.'

The Doctor glared indignantly at him. 'You said you were going to help me!'

'I said nothing of the kind. This contraption is obviously incapable of taking anyone anywhere.'

'If only you would try to use what little intelligence you have, Brigade-Leader.'

'I have no time for fairy stories, Doctor!'

Elizabeth Shaw said, 'If you could give us some proof, Doctor? A demonstration . . .'

'Demonstration?' The Doctor was outraged. 'What do you think I am, a conjuror? How can I give you a demonstration when I haven't got – ' The Doctor broke off. 'Now, wait a moment. It would mean draining the storage unit completely . . .'

The Doctor came to a decision. 'All right. You shall have your demonstration. Stand well back, please.'

The Doctor studied the console for a moment, and then his hands moved rapidly over the controls. The power hum began again, the central column rose and fell, very slowly, and the Doctor and the TARDIS console disappeared.

The Brigade-Leader was left staring at the empty air in astonishment. 'Doctor', he called. 'Doctor, come back!'

A second or two later the Doctor did just that, reappearing as suddenly and mysteriously as he had vanished.

'Well, are you satisfied? Or do you think it was all done with mirrors?'

Elizabeth Shaw said wonderingly. 'What happened? Where were you?'

'A pitiful few seconds into the future,' said the Doctor sadly. He began checking over the console.

Up till now the Brigade-Leader had been too amazed to speak, but as the Doctor reached for the console he shouted, 'Stay away from that!'

The Doctor ignored him. 'Don't be a fool, man, I can't go anywhere. The energy storage unit is completely drained.'

'If the power was reconnected – could you make the journey back?'

'Very possibly. If I reverse the co-ordinates . . .'

'And you could take others with you?'

All at once the Doctor saw the reason for the Brigade-Leader's interest in the TARDIS console. He wanted to use it as a kind of transdimensional lifeboat.

'Certainly not! I can't possibly do that.'

'And why not?'

'It would create a dimensional paradox. There would be a risk of shattering the entire space/time continuum.'

'If you can save yourself, Doctor, you can save us,' said the Brigade-Leader. 'We shall return to central control.'

The voice from the loudspeaker was deep and throaty. *'Doctor Williams,'* it said painfully. *'Doctor Williams . . .'*

Petra Williams stared disbelievingly at the speaker. 'Greg!' she called. 'Greg, I heard a voice from the intercom – it was coming from the drill-head!'

Greg Sutton said uneasily, 'Not a chance. They're all done for in there by now.'

The Doctor, the Brigade-Leader and Section-Leader Shaw came into central control, just as the voice spoke again.

'*Doctor Williams . . . did . . . you . . . not . . . hear . . . me? Raise . . . the shield . . . The . . . manual . . . controls . . . have fused . . . with . . . the heat. Can . . . you . . . let . . . us . . . through?*'

'It's the Director,' whispered Petra Williams. 'We've got to get him out of there.' She moved to a console.

The Doctor pulled her away. 'No . . . no, you mustn't. Believe me, you mustn't raise that heat-shield!'

The Brigade-Leader drew his pistol. 'On the contrary, if the Director has survived he must have found a solution, and we need him out here. Raise the shield, Doctor Williams.'

Helplessly the Doctor watched as Petra operated controls.

With a slow metallic grinding the heat-shield rose – and a disaster-suited figure moved out of the tunnel. It raised its hands and pulled off its helmet to reveal, not Stahlman, but the creature that had once been Stahlman, and was now something far more beast than man. It was the most advanced case of the mutation that the Doctor had yet seen. The face and hands were entirely covered with hair. The whole shape of the jaw had changed and the teeth were great yellow fangs. The eyes glared redly, bestial and savage.

Out of the tunnel behind Stahlman shambled the monstrous creatures that had once been the technicians. With them too the mutation had reached its final stage – accelerated, the Doctor supposed, by the extreme heat. The creatures grouped themselves in a semi circle, behind Stahlman, clearly recognising him as their leader.

Why don't they attack?' whispered the Brigade-Leader.

The Doctor studied the little group of mutants. 'I think they must be acclimatising themselves. It's cooler out here.'

Greg Sutton looked nervously around him. 'Let's get out of here!'

The Brigade-Leader looked round. 'They've covered both entrances!'

'We've got to get to the Brigade-Leader's office,' said the Doctor quietly. 'It's our only chance.'

86

Platoon Under-Leader Benton came running in – and stopped in astonishment at the sight of the ring of mutants.

'Get back, Benton,' shouted the Brigade-Leader.

It was too late. Instinctively Benton raised his automatic rifle and opened fire. The nearest mutant staggered back under the hail of bullets. The others closed in, and one of them tore the rifle from Benton's hands. They held him fast as Stahlman approached, reached out and slowly dragged a hand across Benton's face, leaving a trail of green slime. Benton collapsed, screaming and writhing. The mutants moved almost indifferently away.

While all this was happening the Doctor was far from idle. He could do nothing to help Benton, but his fate made a useful diversion. 'Into the office, all of you,' he shouted.

The Doctor hurried to the console and operated the shield controls. As the shield began to come down he opened a panel and ripped out a handful of wiring, in an attempt to make the process irreversible. Then the Doctor dashed for the office, herding the others in front of him.

Greg Sutton was the last to move. He was staring at Benton's body, and seemed almost inclined to go and help. The Doctor pulled him away. 'No, don't touch him. Don't even go near him! There's nothing you can do.' And he virtually dragged Sutton into the already crowded office, then closed and locked the door behind them.

'We shouldn't have left the poor devil,' protested Sutton. 'Don't mind sacrificing your men, do you , Brigade-Leader?'

'Believe me, Mr Sutton,' said the Doctor gently. 'There's nothing we can do.'

'Not now, we can't. Those things have probably killed him.'

'Worse than that. They've made him one of them.'

'Why did you shut them off from the drill-head?' asked Petra Williams.

'To keep them from the heat. The hotter it is, the stronger they grow.'

Sutton mopped his forehead. 'If it gets any hotter in here they won't have to attack. We'll just shrivel up.'

The Brigade-Leader too was sweating, more from nerves

87

than from heat. His voice when he spoke was tense, almost hysterical. 'Well, Doctor, I don't think your precious vehicle is going to be much use to anyone now!'

Sutton stared at him. 'Vehicle? What are you talking about?'

'The Doctor has a device,' explained Elizabeth Shaw. 'Something that could get him out of here.'

The Brigade-Leader laughed almost hysterically. 'Just the Doctor, of course. No one else.'

'Look', said Sutton despairingly. 'Will someone tell me what's going on?'

He wasn't really much the wiser when the explanations were over.

'So you see,' concluded the Brigade-Leader, 'We're all supposed to sacrifice our lives so the Doctor can get back to his other world.'

'We haven't got any lives to sacrifice,' said Elizabeth Shaw crisply. 'It's only a matter of time for us now.'

Petra Williams looked at Sutton. 'What do you think, Greg?'

'I think it's the weirdest story I've ever heard,' said Sutton frankly. 'But I'm on your side, Doc. Might as well try to do something useful.'

Elizabeth Shaw said, 'I'm afraid you're out-voted Brigade-Leader.'

'Really?' The Brigade-Leader laughed. 'It doesn't actually matter very much, does it? Since we're all trapped in here anyway.'

The Doctor cleared his throat. 'As a matter of fact, I do have a plan for getting us out of here. It all depends on those creatures out there . . .'

The Doctor's explanation was interrupted when one of the creatures outside smashed its fist through the glass window in the office door.

11

Escape Plan

Immediately there was pandemonium. Everyone leaped back. The Brigade-Leader drew his revolver and began firing frantically through the window. Quite unaffected, the arm flailed about as if seeking a victim.

'Don't touch it anyone,' yelled the Doctor. 'And don't let it touch you!'

The door began to shudder as heavy bodies hurled themselves against it. Through the shattered window, the Doctor could see the mutants milling round outside the door. They would smash it down by their sheer weight very soon.

Looking round, the Doctor was vastly relieved to see a fire-extinguisher clipped to the wall. He grabbed it and sent a stream of CO_2 vapour through the broken window. The effect was immediate. With angry screams and roars the monsters began falling back. Soon all was silent – except for the faint sounds of the creatures grunting and shuffling outside.

'We've got to keep them out,' said the Brigade-Leader worriedly.

The Doctor put down his fire-extinguisher. 'They won't attack again just yet. I think they'll try again when it gets a bit hotter.'

'How long have we got?' asked Elizabeth Shaw.

'Oh, a good ten minutes!' said the Doctor cheerfully.

'Just now you were talking about a plan, Doctor,' said Sutton. 'What plan?'

'If we're to get power to the TARDIS console, we've got to connect it to the reactor.'

'If there's any power left, said Petra gloomily.

The Doctor whipped a handkerchief from his pocket and

held it up to the air-conditioning grille in the wall. The handkerchief fluttered. 'You see? The air-conditioning's still working – so power is still being produced.'

'Only the bare minimum,' said Petra. 'The reactor must still be functioning on robot control.'

'Can we boost the output?'

Petra considered. 'In an emergency like this, the master switch shuts down the main reactor banks automatically.'

'But it could be reconnected?'

Sutton had been listening with keen interest. 'Thing is, Doctor, the master switch is in main control. How do we get past that lot out there?'

The Doctor tapped the fire-extinguisher. 'Well, we do have a weapon against them.'

'One extinguisher won't last for ever,' Petra said. 'Resetting the master control could be a long job – especially if it's been damaged.'

The Doctor looked nonplussed for a moment, then he brightened. 'There are lots more fire-extinguishers in central control.'

'If we can get to them,' said Sutton. 'Hey, wait a minute. I'm a flaming idiot – I rigged up an emergency hose connection to the coolant pipes. That stuff's under pressure too and it's just as cold as CO_2. Doctor, there's a monster-size fire-extinguisher just waiting for you out there.'

'Right,' said the Doctor briskly. 'We'll fight our way into central control using this extinguisher here. While Mr Sutton holds the creatures off with his coolant hose, I'll operate the master switch.'

There was a threatening roar. A savage hairy face appeared in the shattered window. The mutants were massing for a second attack. Sutton grabbed the extinguisher. The weakened door collapsed inwards and mutants flooded into the room, jamming the doorway in their eagerness to get inside.

'Right, fire!' shouted the Doctor.

Sutton poured CO_2 gas over the group of mutants. Immediately they fell back, screeching and roaring in protest. Sutton led the trapped party out into central control, clearing the way with the extinguisher.

The main control area was in semi-darkness now with only the dim working lights still burning. The heat was stifling and the air was full of smoke. The whole place was vibrating with the deep dull roaring that came from the drill-head. In the shadowy recesses of the huge control area, mutants lurked – waiting, moving uneasily to and fro, and occasionally screeching angrily.

Handing the extinguisher to the Brigade-Leader, Sutton led them over to a huge coolant pipe running down one of the walls. Reaching behind it he pulled out a long coil of thick metallic hose already connected to the pipe by a valve. He set to work to open the valve. It was jammed by the heat, and he began struggling to free it.

Everyone was watching Sutton. Nobody saw one of the mutants moving stealthily towards them.

'Hurry up, Sutton,' growled the Brigade-Leader.

'I'm going as fast as I can. Everything's red hot!'

'I can't breathe in here!'

'Then stop talking so much,' advised the Doctor briskly.

Suddenly Elizabeth Shaw spotted the approaching monster. 'Look out!'

The Brigade-Leader swung round, and opened fire with the extinguisher. The creature fell back screeching angrily.

'That's enough,' ordered the Doctor. 'Don't waste it!'

The Brigade-Leader ignored him, drenching the mutant in a stream of CO_2.

The Doctor thumped him on the shoulder. '*I said that's enough!*'

The monster had collapsed by now. It rolled over face upwards, twitched and then lay still.

The Doctor peered down at it. 'It's Stahlman. Or it was.'

'Is he dead?' asked Petra Williams.

'It may be just paralysed. It might come to again as the temperature rises.'

'Come on, Sutton,' said the Brigade-Leader. 'Get that coolant flowing.'

Sutton looked up. 'I can't. It's seized up.'

The Doctor looked round and spotted a discarded tool-kit. He made a quick dash, grabbed a crowbar more or less at random and dashed back to Sutton. 'Here, try this!'

Sutton slipped the crowbar into the valve wheel and heaved. It still refused to turn. The Doctor came and added his strength to Sutton's. With agonising slowness the wheel began to yield.

Anxiously watching their progress, the Brigade-Leader failed to register that the mutants were edging closer.

'Look out!' shouted Elizabeth Shaw again.

The Brigade-Leader opened fire, driving the mutants back with the icy spray. The moment it touched their bodies they screeched in agony and recoiled. Soon the area around the little group was clear again, at least for the moment.

'We've got it!' shouted Sutton. A thin wisp of coolant vapour was coming from the nozzle of the hose. Sutton adjusted the nozzle control and the wisp became an icy stream. Satisfied he turned it down again.

As usual, the Doctor took command. 'All right, Brigade-Leader. You cover the ladies to the exit. I'll be out as soon as I've reconnected the master switch.'

The Brigade-Leader took a firm grip on his extinguisher. 'Very well, ladies, let's get moving.'

They moved slowly towards the door. The Brigade-Leader swung the extinguisher to and fro, sending out a blast of CO_2 whenever one of the mutants ventured too near.

'Right, Doctor, let's get on with it,' said Sutton.

The Doctor made his way over to the main power console. Sutton followed, paying out the hose.

Even outside the control building there was no relief from the stifling heat. The whole sky was red now and everything shimmered and danced in the heat haze. From the distance came the rumble of volcanic eruptions.

'It's just as hot out here,' grumbled the Brigade-Leader. 'I still can't breathe properly. Well, come on, no use hanging about.'

'We shall wait for the others,' said Elizabeth Shaw.

The Brigade-Leader looked round uneasily. 'But we ought to get right away from here.'

'You go if you want to,' said Petra Williams. 'We're staying here.'

The Doctor was working absorbedly on the master switch. 'The heat's made a bit of a mess of this.'

'It's making a mess of me,' said Sutton.

'You could always join the others outside.'

'Oh, I'll hang around a bit longer,' said Sutton casually. A mutant was sneaking closer and he sent it screeching back with a quick blast of coolant vapour. 'The natives are getting restless again. How are you making out?'

'Slow but sure.'

'When you get back to the other place, Doc, how do you reckon to stop them drilling?'

'I don't know . . . One or two people might listen – like Sir Keith.'

'He's dead,' said Sutton automatically.

'In your world, yes, Mr Sutton. But in that other world – maybe not . . . In any case, time's running out for them.'

Sutton looked round uneasily. 'I think time's running out here too, Doc.' The encircling monsters were edging closer.

The Doctor straightened up. 'There, that's it. I just hope it works. Trouble is, there's no means of testing it, not until power is channelled from the reactor.' The Doctor looked round, and saw that they were now surrounded by a ring of mutants, steadily closing in. 'Yes,' said the Doctor thoughtfully. 'I really think we ought to be getting out of here. Shall we go, Mr Sutton?'

'I thought you'd never ask!'

The monsters attacked. Sutton swept the coolant round in a great arc, driving them back. The Doctor snatched an extinguisher from the wall and joined in the attack. As they came near the door, the attack of the mutants was pressed home more and more vigorously, as if they were determined to prevent their escape. Inch by inch, the Doctor and Sutton fought their way out. The most dangerous moment came when Sutton's coolant hose would stretch no further. Protected only by the Doctor's extinguisher, they made a last desperate dash for the door, reaching it with only inches to spare.

As they ran down the front steps the mutants fell back, not caring to leave the shelter of the building.

The Brigade-Leader and the two girls ran forward to meet them. 'We'd better hurry, Doctor,' said the Brigade-Leader. 'It's quite a way to the reactor.'

The Doctor looked round. 'Yes, but it's not all that far to where I left Bessie. Come on!' He led them off at a run.

In the control centre the creature that had once been Stahlman was recovering from the blast of CO_2. Slowly it got to its feet.

Somewhat overloaded, Bessie screeched to a halt outside the nuclear reactor. The Doctor and his party jumped out and ran inside the building. They paused just inside the doorway.

'Section-Leader, check the inner corridors,' said the Brigade-Leader.

She nodded and moved away.

'Mr Sutton and I had better start work on the other end of the power connections. How long will you need here, Doctor Williams?'

Petra shrugged. 'It's hard to say. I'll have to re-route the entire electrical system before I can boost the power.'

'Well, just do the best you can.'

Elizabeth Shaw returned from her reconnaissance. 'Everything seems clear. What about the Brigade-Leader and me? Can we do anything?'

'I'm afraid not,' said the Doctor gently. 'You'd better wait here.' He turned to Sutton. 'We'll need tools and a lot of heavy-duty cable.'

'Riggers' store,' said Sutton. 'We pass it on the way to your hut.'

'Let's get on with it then.'

Suddenly there was a distant rumble and for a moment the whole building seemed to shake.

Elizabeth Shaw looked worriedly at the Doctor. 'What's happening?'

'It's an earthquake – a whole chain of earthquakes.'

'Getting nearer,' said Petra.

'Come on,' shouted the Doctor, and he and Sutton ran from the building. They jumped into Bessie, and the Doctor drove away.

The Stahlman mutant came to the doorway of central control. It paused for a moment, as if testing the temperature. Then it moved outside. Others followed.

In the main switch room Petra Williams worked desperately on the controls. The Brigade-Leader and Section-Leader Shaw stood looking on, all the more impatient because there was nothing they could do to help.

Elizabeth Shaw said thoughtfully, 'I wonder if those creatures are venturing out of the control area yet?'

'Quite possible,' said the Brigade-Leader gloomily. 'It's getting hotter all the time.' He looked irritably at Petra. 'How long is all that going to take you?'

'I don't know,' said Petra calmly. She went on working.

'Can't you hurry it up?'

'Not if I'm to do it properly.'

'You must hurry! We are running very short of time.'

Petra looked up. 'Brigade-Leader, I am trying to carry out a complex scientific task under almost impossible conditions. You will not help matters by bullying me.'

'You are insolent, Doctor Williams!'

'Am I, Brigade-Leader? Perhaps it's time you learned that some problems are not solvable by brute force and terror.'

Elizabeth Shaw drew the Brigade-Leader away. 'Better let her get on with it. We're in her hands.'

He nodded. 'We've got to get the power through to that hut. It's our only chance to escape.'

'But the Doctor said he couldn't take anyone else.'

'Naturally, Section-Leader. Do you think he wants to help us? He's only concerned with his own safety.'

Elizabeth Shaw shook her head. 'I think he was telling the truth – just as he has been all along.'

The Brigade-Leader rested a hand on his revolver. 'When the time comes, he will take us, Section-Leader. He will have no choice.'

12

Doomsday

Greg Sutton opened the doors to the Doctor's hut and the Doctor drove Bessie inside, parking the little car in its usual place before the console. He jumped out and began examining the controls.

Sutton was staring at the console in amazement. 'So this is the contraption, is it? I thought it would be a bit more impressive than that.'

'What did you expect? Some sort of space rocket with Batman at the controls?'

Sutton grinned. 'Maybe. And that thing brought you here, did it?'

'It wasn't exactly a journey in your sense of the word. It sort of slipped me sideways into your dimension.'

'And now it's going to take you back?'

'Well, theoretically,' said the Doctor. 'Just fix the cable to that connection down there for me would you?'

Sutton examined the connection point and then looked up. 'I hate to tell you but we're never going to get enough juice through this. It'll blow in the first few seconds.'

The Doctor said gently. 'A few seconds, Mr Sutton, is all I need.'

The Brigade-Leader strode up and down the main switch-room, occasionally glancing worriedly at Petra Williams who seemed to have taken most of the power console to pieces.

'Are you making any progress, Doctor Williams?'

'Some. But I'm worried about the relay circuits. They don't seem to be operating properly. I'm trying to rig up a by-pass. The reactor is still functioning, but it could go at any moment.'

'I am well aware of that. You must hurry!'

'I've already told you – I'm hurrying as much as I can.'

There was another earthquake tremor, much nearer this time. Once again the room shook. The Brigade-Leader clutched at the door frame, visibly terrified.

'It's all right, Brigade-Leader,' said Elizabeth Shaw almost mockingly. 'We're still here.'

'I don't like your tone, Section-Leader. These earthquakes are getting closer. I'm thinking of the safety of us all.'

'Yes, of course.'

There was another rumble and the whole building shuddered.

The Brigade-Leader's voice was panicky. 'We've got to get out of here.'

'I shall leave when the work is finished,' said Petra calmly. 'You may leave now if you wish.'

He glared angrily at her. 'Silence! Carry on with your work.'

Elizabeth Shaw said quietly, 'Wouldn't it be better for us to leave now?'

He shook his head. 'That craft of the Doctor's is our only chance. It works – you saw for yourself.'

'Do you really think you can force him to take us with him? He's not the sort of man you can frighten.'

'Once the thing's working we'll just take it over.'

'We don't know how to work it.'

The Brigade-Leader was deaf to all objections. 'Doctor Williams can operate it then, she's a scientist.'

'That device is beyond all our comprehension. No one but the Doctor can operate it, I'm sure of that.'

'Then we shall have to persuade him to operate it for us.'

'And if he refuses?'

'If the Doctor tries to leave us here to die, Section-Leader, I shall make sure that he dies first!'

In the hut the Doctor and Sutton were working busily.

'If we do get you back, Doctor,' said Sutton grimly, 'you'd better make darned sure your people do stop drilling. I'd hate to think I was doing all this work for nothing.'

'I shall do my best, I assure you! We can connect up the cable now.'

'Then cross our fingers and trust to luck?'

'We are relying on skill, Mr Sutton, not luck,' said the Doctor reproachfully. But he crossed his fingers all the same.

Wearily Petra straightened up.

'Finished?' asked Elizabeth Shaw.

'I think so. I just have to switch on and preset the power controls.'

'How do we know when the Doctor's ready for the power?'

'It doesn't matter. The power won't flow until the Doctor switches on.'

'At which point we may all go up in smoke,' said the Brigade-Leader acidly.

Petra Williams gave the console a final check. 'I've done all I can now. We'll just have to see.' She pulled the main switch. Nothing happened.

'What's happened?' demanded the Brigade-Leader.

'Nothing. There must still be a fault.'

'So, you've been wasting our time.'

Petra ignored him. 'I'll just have to check all the wiring again.'

The Doctor and Sutton were waiting for the power that did not come.

'Maybe something's happened to them?' said Sutton uneasily.

'We must try to be patient, Mr Sutton.'

'If those explosions reach the nuclear reactor . . .'

'I know,' said the Doctor gently. 'I know.'

There was another colossal explosion, different in character, and nearer this time.

'That's coming from the drill shaft,' gasped the Brigade-Leader.

Elizabeth Shaw said calmly. 'The shaft must be splitting open.'

'Look out!' shouted the Brigade-Leader suddenly.

Both girls looked up. A mutant stood in the doorway – the mutant that had once been Stahlman.

The Brigade-Leader snatched up a fire-extinguisher and pulled the lever. The extinguisher was empty. He drew his revolver and stepped in front of the mutant. It lashed out at him screeching angrily.

He backed away, luring it from the doorway. 'Get out, you two,' he called. 'Just get out!'

The two girls ran to the door, the mutant swung round – and the Brigade-Leader emptied the contents of his revolver into it at point-blank range. Screeching, the mutant fell to the ground. Leaping over the body, the Brigade-Leader ran from the room.

Sutton was peering into the explosion-wrecked landscape outside the hut. 'No sign of them – nothing.'

The Doctor sighed. 'Well, that would appear to be that. I doubt if they would have listened to me anyway.' Sadly he patted the console.

The Brigade-Leader, Petra and Elizabeth Shaw were running for their lives, snarling mutants at their heels. The creatures were pouring from the drill-head now. So great was the heat that they could move freely in the open. The fugitives had only one advantage: their superior speed – all the mutants seemed to move with that same awkward, stumbling motion – and they soon began to leave their pursuers behind.

Sutton saw them approaching from the doorway of the hut. 'They're coming! All three of them.'

Seconds later, the Brigade-Leader and the two girls dashed into the hut.

'Well done, Petra,' said Greg. Then he saw her face. 'What's the matter?'

Petra turned to the Doctor. 'I'm sorry, I couldn't get the power through. I did all I could.'

'Yes, of course you did.'

Sutton slumped wearily against the wall. 'Well, we tried, eh, Doc?'

'No one can do more than that, Mr Sutton.'

99

The Brigade-Leader said mockingly, 'All very philosophical, Doctor. "I know you tried, thank you very much." That's very cosy.'

'Hysteria won't help us, Brigade-Leader.'

'Nothing will help us now. Things will blow at any moment – we'll be roasted alive!'

'Look what's happening to our hard man,' jeered Sutton. 'You were tough enough with a gang of thugs behind you. How do you like it on your own? You're finished, Brigade-Leader!'

'I can still deal with you, Sutton,' snarled the Brigade-Leader. He drew his revolver.

'With that? Even if you had the guts, you'd be doing me a favour.'

The Brigade-Leader pulled the trigger again and again – and every time the hammer clicked on an empty chamber.

'I don't need a gun to settle with you, Sutton,' he grunted and hurled himself upon the engineer, knocking him to the ground. They rolled over and over, fighting savagely, clawing at each other like wild beasts.

There came another volcanic rumble, so intense that they were literally thrown apart. The Doctor stepped between them. 'Listen to that! Do you want to end your lives fighting like animals?'

Sutton jumped up and stared around him. 'Where's Petra?'

'She's gone back to the switch room,' said Elizabeth Shaw. 'She wanted to have another go at getting the power through.'

'The idiot! I'd better go after her.'

The Doctor said, 'I'll come with you.

'No, Doctor. She might just make it – and if she does, you've got to be here.' He ran from the hut.

Greg Sutton ran blindly through the red glare of the nightmare landscape, the ground trembling beneath his feet. Somehow he succeeded in avoiding the wandering mutants, and arrived in the switch room – to find Petra calmly working, doing her best to ignore the mutant body on the floor.

'Petra, what do you think you're doing?' he shouted.

'I've nearly finished, Greg. I'd nearly finished when we ran out of here. I only need a few more minutes.'

'You were crazy to risk coming back!' He looked down at the mutant. 'What about this thing?'

'It's all right. He's dead.'

'He might not have been! Those things are hard to kill. All right, you get on, now you're here. I'll keep an eye out.' Sutton went to the door and peered out through the heat-hazed landscape. Suddenly he heard a scream from behind him and whirled round.

Seemingly indestructible, the Stahlman mutant had staggered to its feet and was lurching towards Petra. Snatching up a fire-extinguisher from a clip outside the door, Sutton blasted the mutant at close range. Already weakened by the Brigadier's bullets it gave one last terrifying screech and crashed to the ground.

Sutton ran to Petra. 'Are you all right?'

'Yes, I think so,' A little shakily, Petra went back to work. Minutes later she looked up. 'There, that should do it.' She threw the switch. There was a hum of power and needles on the high-voltage dials flickered and started to climb.

'It's working!' said Petra.

Sutton hugged her. 'Well done! We'd better get back to the hut!'

The Doctor was hunched over his console studying the instruments. 'I'm geting power through!' he called excitedly.

Elizabeth Shaw said, 'That's splendid, Doctor.'

The Brigade-Leader was quietly re-loading his gun.

Petra and Greg Sutton ran into the hut.

'Well done, Doctor Williams,' said the Doctor. 'Well done!'

'You'd better hurry, Doctor,' warned Petra. 'The power won't hold out for long!'

'Long enough, I hope,' said the Brigade-Leader.

Something in his tone made the Doctor look up. He saw the revolver in the Brigade-Leader's hand.

'You are going to take me with you, Doctor.'

101

'I can't take you with me,' said the Doctor desperately. 'It's impossible.'

The Brigade-Leader raised his revolver. 'I advise you to try.'

'Don't you see, I can't. I literally can't. There would be a cosmic disaster.'

'Believe me, you are not going to leave us behind.'

'Do you think I want to do it? I'd give anything to be able to save you all – but I can't!'

'Never mind the gun,' called Sutton. 'It's not loaded, remember?'

The Brigade-Leader fired a shot close to the Doctor's head. 'We all helped you, Doctor. We've every right to go. I'll give you until a count of three. One . . .'

'I'm afraid you'll have to shoot me, Brigade-Leader. Nothing will make me take you.'

'Two . . . three.'

A shot rang out – and the Brigade-Leader fell. The astonished Doctor turned and saw Elizabeth Shaw, holstering a revolver.

'Go on, Doctor! Go now!'

'Get on with it!' shouted Sutton.

The Doctor's hands moved over the controls. There was a wheezing, groaning sound, and the centre column rose and fell. But the console and the Doctor didn't disappear.

There was a final, shattering explosion from outside.

The drill tower and the entire control centre erupted in smoke and flames. A great crack appeared where it had once stood, and red hot lava began flooding out. The air was filled with the dying screams of the mutants who had been huddled around the complex, and were now devoured, like fiery sacrifices to their savage god.

The Doctor was still working frantically.

'Hurry, Doctor!' shouted Elizabeth Shaw. 'Hurry!'

Suddenly Petra gasped, 'Look!' She pointed through the open door. An enormous wall of glowing lava was rolling like a tidal wave towards the little hut.

Suddenly the TARDIS noise grew louder. They all

turned and saw that the TARDIS console was vibrating. The centre column rose and fell – and suddenly the console, the Doctor, and even the little car, all disappeared. Before the sea of red hot lava engulfed the hut, its victims had just a few seconds to realise that their sacrifice might not have been in vain.

13

Return to Danger

On that Earth which the Doctor had left, and to which he was now trying to return, the Earth that was endangered but not yet destroyed, matters at the Stahlman project had reached a very bad state indeed.

Brigadier Alastair Lethbridge-Stewart was an angry, frustrated, and extremely worried man.

First there were the outbreaks of this recessive mutation, which turned soldiers and scientists alike into savage beasts. The Brigadier was uneasily aware that some of its victims were still at liberty. If they infected others . . .

Then there was the disappearance of the Doctor, a typically inconsiderate piece of behaviour, at the time when he was most needed.

And now there was a second disappearance – that of Sir Keith Gold. He had gone to London, kept his appointment with the Minister, and according to one of the Minister's aides, had a very successful meeting. He had then set off on the return journey to the complex – but had never arrived back. The Brigadier had checked with the police and with hospitals – there had been no accident involving Sir Keith on any conceivable route between London and the complex.

Finally, and indeed continually, there was the behaviour of Professor Stahlman. The Brigadier had had one brief and acrimonious interview with Stahlman, achieved only by sending Benton to more or less drag him to his office. The Brigadier had requested that in view of the Doctor's and Sir Keith's anxieties, drilling should be suspended, or at least slowed down until one or both of them returned. He had been met with an angry and contemptuous refusal. Stahlman was insistent that penetration-zero would be reached on schedule – his schedule. With Sir Keith still away, there was no one to stop him.

Liz Shaw was equally worried. With the Doctor gone there was little she could do – Stahlman certainly had no use for her assistance or advice. She spent quite a lot of her time pottering about in the Doctor's hut, hoping that by some miracle he would return. Sometimes Sergeant Benton or Greg Sutton would pop in for a chat, but most of the time she was on her own.

Opening the hut door to begin one of these lonely vigils, it took Liz a moment to register that Bessie was back in her place. Beyond Bessie was the TARDIS console, and lying at the foot of the console was the Doctor.

'Doctor!' she called delightedly. She ran and knelt beside him. The Doctor's body was limp and motionless. He was breathing, but that was about all.

Suddenly Liz heard voices outside the hut. She jumped to her feet and ran to the still-open door. Sergeant Benton was passing, talking to one of his foot-patrols.

'Sergeant Benton!' she called. 'Over here!'

Benton came running into the hut. He stopped in the doorway in delighted astonishment. 'It's the Doctor!'

'I can see that,' said Liz rather unkindly. 'Go and tell the Brigadier.'

'Right away, miss!' Benton set off at a run.

Liz felt for the pulse in the Doctor's neck. It was very faint, but it was there . . .

Central control was filled with the steady roar from the drill-head, operating at near-maximum revs.

The digital clock read 03.22: three hours twenty-two minutes to penetration-zero. Professor Stahlman was telling Petra Williams how things could be speeded up even further. 'It's perfectly simple, Petra. We boost all the power circuits to maximum load. That will give us a further acceleration of . . . 3.6 per cent.'

Petra said nothing but her face showed her concern.

Stahlman frowned. 'Well? Perhaps you see some flaw in my calculations?'

'Of course not, Professor. But we're already twelve per

cent over the planned acceleration rate. Another three will take us over all the safety margins.'

'Safety margins are for old women, Petra – like Sir Keith. I know what I'm doing. Pass on my instructions.' He moved away.

Petra turned and found Greg Sutton at her elbow. 'You look worried,' he said bluntly.

'Professor Stahlman has ordered a further acceleration. Three per cent.'

Sutton was outraged. 'He can't do that! We're pushing the safety limits already. I'm going to have a word with him.'

Petra shook her head. 'Don't. It won't do any good. He usually listens to me, but . . .'

'But not any more, eh? Face it, Petra, he's losing his grip.'

Petra's instincts of loyalty were still strong. 'Professor Stahlman has been working on this project for years. He must know what he's doing.'

'He can still make mistakes – and if he makes one at this stage it will be a lulu.'

'Greg – let me talk to him first.'

Sutton grinned and patted her on the shoulder. 'Right! You soften him up, and I'll come in for the kill.'

The Brigadier was just coming out of his office when he was almost knocked flying by Sergeant Benton. Benton skidded to a halt just in time and saluted. 'Sir!'

The Brigadier raised an eyebrow. 'Well, Benton?'

'It's the Doctor, sir. He's back.'

'What? Where is he?'

'In his hut, sir. Miss Shaw's with him.'

Greg Sutton who was standing nearby had been listening with keen interest. 'What was all that about, Brigadier?'

'Nothing of importance, Mr Sutton.'

'Come off it. He said something about the Doc.'

'The Doctor appears to have turned up again.'

'Hey, that's great. How did he get back in here?'

'Probably the same way he got out, Mr Sutton. I'd be obliged if you wouldn't mention this to anyone just yet – and particularly not to Professor Stahlman.'

Sutton grinned. 'Don't worry. I want to get Stahlman in a good mood!'

At the drill-head Petra was having little success.

'My dear Petra,' said Stahlman impatiently. 'Much as I value your advice, I must remind you that you are not . . . that I am . . . in control . . . in control . . .' Stahlman broke off, staring fixedly at the drill-shaft. He clamped his hands to his ears as if to shut out some intolerable noise.

Petra was alarmed. 'Professor Stahlman, are you all right?'

He recovered himself. 'It's nothing . . . a slight headache . . .'

'You really ought to go to the sick-bay.'

I am perfectly all right, Petra.

It was at this unfortunate moment that Greg Sutton appeared to make his appeal. He began with his usual bluntness. 'This accelerated drilling just isn't on, Professor.'

'I see,' said Stahlman icily. 'Now someone else is about to tell me how to run my project.'

Sutton ploughed on. 'We ought to be slowing down at this stage, not forcing the pace.'

'The drilling will continue at the pace I decide!'

Sutton tried to change his approach. 'Listen, you've spent years on this project, right? What's all the rush during these last few hours? Since you've waited so long . . .'

Stahlman stared fixedly at him. 'We must reach penetration-zero at the earliest possible moment. Every second is vital.' Once again he clamped his hands over his ears.

Sutton looked hard at him. 'I reckon you need a rest, Professor.'

Stahlman turned to Petra and said stiffly. 'I do not intend to discuss the matter further. See that my orders are carried out.' He turned and walked through the tunnel to central control.

Sutton gave Petra a rueful look. 'I thought you were going to soften him up!'

'He just won't listen,' she said desperately. 'I think he's

ill, Greg. He had some kind of attack.'

'I know, I saw. This whole thing's getting too much for him, Petra. He's cracking up!'

A camp bed had been set up in a corner of the Doctor's hut, and his long thin body lay stretched out on it. Liz had thought it wiser not to move him too far. She was examining him now, watched by the Brigadier. She looked up. 'Hearts beating steadily . . .'

'Both of them?'

'Yes.'

The Brigadier looked down at the Doctor with a mixture of exasperation and concern. 'Then what's the matter with him?'

Liz shrugged. 'Some sort of coma.'

'How long before he comes out of it?'

'Impossible to say. A few hours . . . days . . . months.'

'Months!' The Brigadier was horrified.

Liz said, 'Some people never come out at all.'

'I'll send for a doctor.'

'I happen to be a doctor, Brigadier, remember?'

Liz Shaw had so many scientific qualifications that it was easy to forget that there was a medical degree amongst them.

The Brigadier slapped his leg with his cane, impatient to be doing something. 'Shouldn't we at least get him to a hospital?'

'It would be dangerous to move him at all.'

'We can't just leave him here.'

'Why not? It's quiet.' Liz nodded to some electric heaters rigged up by Benton's men. 'We can keep him warm.'

'I really think he needs proper medical attention, Miss Shaw.'

'I'll look after him,' said Liz fiercely.

The Brigadier bowed to her determination. 'Very well.' He looked down at the Doctor's still form. 'There'll be a row if Stahlman finds out he's back.'

'Stahlman doesn't have to know, does he?' Liz studied the Doctor's peaceful face. 'He was like this when I first met him, remember? I think it's his way of protecting himself against tremendous strain. He'll wake up – when he's ready.'

Greg Sutton drew a deep breath, fixed an ingratiating smile on his rugged features and went up to Professor Stahlman, determined that this time he would handle the old boy properly. 'If you could spare me a moment, Professor?'

Stahlman ignored him, and went on checking instrument readings against the figures on his clip-board.

Sutton forced himself to go on in the same humble tones. 'I've just been checking the emergency flange on number 2 output pipe.'

Stahlman spoke without looking up. 'It was repaired some time ago.'

'Well, they didn't do a very good job. At the speed we're drilling, that flange could blow at any moment.'

'And what do you suggest?'

'If we slow down the drilling rate, I could get a proper job done.'

Stahlman looked up. 'So! Another transparent excuse for delay!'

Sutton forgot all his good resolutions. 'Excuse, nothing! Carry on at this rate, and this place will go sky high before you ever reach penetration-zero! Look, I'm trying to help you. I'm supposed to be an adviser.'

'Oh yes! One of Sir Keith's little army of experts. Well, I don't need your advice, Mr Sutton. That ridiculous Doctor has gone, Sir Keith himself has gone. Why don't you follow their example? Then, perhaps, we could make some progress.'

As Stahlman moved away Greg Sutton shouted, 'Don't worry, I'll do just that. As far as I'm concerned you can blow yourself to kingdom come.' He stood there fuming, recognising that his attempt at being diplomatic had been a dismal failure.

Petra Williams said, 'Are you serious? You're really convinced there'll be a blow-up?'

'I'd lay odds on it. If I can't do anything else, I can save my own neck. Why don't you come with me?'

'I've got to stay, Greg, you know that.'

He shook his head. 'Loyal to the last, eh?'

'Greg, I wish you'd change your mind about leaving.'

'Why?'

'If anything does go wrong, I'd like to think you were here. I've got used to having you around.'

Sutton ran his fingers through his close-cropped hair. 'Well, what do you know? Maybe I haven't been wasting my time here after all . . .'

There was the sudden clamour of an alarm from the drill-head.

Inside the drill-head, the flange on number 2 output pipe had burst. Thick heavy vapours were drifting from it and there was an oozing of green slime. Mixed with the hooting of the alarm there was a curious screeching sound . . .

The Brigadier was shouting into the internal telephone.

'Control? This is Lethbridge-Stewart here. What's happening?' He listened. 'Yes, yes, go on . . . How serious?'

While the Brigadier was talking, the Doctor began twisting and muttering, as if roused from his coma by the noise of the alarms.

'Number 2 output pipe's blown,' he muttered. 'Very dangerous . . .'

Liz leaned over him. 'Doctor? Can you hear me? What is it?'

'Number 2 output pipe,' said the Doctor again. 'Very dangerous. Number 2 output pipe has blown . . .'

Putting down the phone, the Brigadier turned round in astonishment. 'How on earth did he know that? The emergency flange has just blown on number 2 output pipe – it's only just happened!'

'Listen,' said Liz.

The Doctor was muttering again. 'Only thing to do . . . reverse all systems. Reverse all systems immediately . . .'

The Brigadier shook his head. 'Delirious, poor chap!'

'Is he? He knew about the blowout – almost as if he was expecting it.' She leaned over the Doctor. 'Can you hear me? Doctor!'

The Doctor had sunk back into his coma.

'Keep an eye on him, will you, Brigadier?' said Liz. 'I'm going to central control!'

By the time Liz reached central control everyone was close to panic – everyone but Stahlman.

'Keep calm,' he bellowed, his voice rising above the howl of alarm. 'This is only a minor emergency. It can be contained.'

'Please, Professor,' begged Petra. 'Close down the drilling.'

'No. Positively not.'

'You'd better do something quickly, Professor,' warned Sutton. 'This place is about to bust wide open!'

Stahlman glared round angrily. 'Have those riggers arrived yet?'

'Look,' said Sutton desperately. 'An army of riggers isn't going to get you out of this one!'

Already frightened technicians were pouring out of the drill-head tunnel. Stahlman ran angrily towards them. 'Get back, all of you! Get back to your posts!'

'Just look at him!' yelled Sutton. 'He isn't even trying to find a solution!'

Petra looked at him in anguish. 'Is there one?'

Liz Shaw came running up. 'What would happen if all the systems were reversed?'

Petra stared at her. 'What?'

'Reverse all the systems!'

'Wait a minute,' said Greg Sutton suddenly. 'That's not such a crazy idea! I've seen it done before, with an oil shaft in Arabia. Push the coolant down the output pipes, and drag up the debris from the bottom of the shaft through the input pipes . . .'

'And reverse the vortex,' said Liz. 'It's a possibility – theoretically.'

'Professor Stahlman would never allow it,' said Petra slowly.

'Just do it,' urged Liz.

'That's right,' said Greg Sutton. 'Well, how about it, Petra?'

Petra Williams looked from one to the other of them. 'All right!' She turned and ran towards the control consoles.

14

The Last Mutation

A short time later, things were back to something like normal in central control. Technicians were back at their posts, the alarm siren had stopped its shrieking, and the readings on the pressure gauges were falling back to something nearer the acceptable limits – though they were still far too high for Greg Sutton's liking.

He looked round the control room with cautious satisfaction. 'Well, it seems to be working. That was a pretty good idea of yours, Miss Shaw.'

'It wasn't my idea.'

Sutton looked at her. 'Then whose – no, don't tell me. The Doctor! The Brigadier said he was back.'

'That's right. The Doctor,' said Liz. She left the control room.

Professor Stahlman was less happy with the way the emergency had been handled. 'You reversed all systems? I gave no such orders, Petra.'

'No Professor,' said Petra steadily. 'I did.'

'Even you, Petra,' said Stahlman sadly. 'Even you.' He turned away.

'Doctor?' called the voice. 'Doctor, are you all right?'

The Doctor opened his eyes and saw a face hovering above him. It looked a little blurred at first, then his vision cleared.

'Liz? It is Liz?'

'That's right.'

And it was Liz, the Doctor saw with relief. The auburn-haired, brightly dressed Liz he knew so well – not the black-haired cold-faced uniformed Section-Leader Shaw, whose mind had been formed by a Fascist state. Yet she had sacrificed herself to save him, the Doctor remembered, together with the other Sutton and the other Petra.

The Doctor heard another, even more familiar voice. 'How are you, Doctor?'

He looked up. There was the Brigadier, immaculately uniformed as usual, without eyepatch or scar, and with that neatly clipped military moustache.

'You know, Brigadier,' said the Doctor thoughtfully, 'you really do look better with your moustache.'

The Brigadier looked at Liz. 'Poor chap's delirious.'

The Doctor struggled to sit up.

'You really ought to lie down for a bit longer,' said Liz anxiously. 'You've been unconscious for quite some time.'

'I am well aware of that,' said the Doctor crisply. He was taking his own pulse. 'Hmm, seventy – more or less normal.' He put a hand first to one side of his chest and then the other. 'Both hearts ticking away nicely. Right-hand one's a fraction fast, but then, that's only to be expected, eh?'

'Where did you go to?' asked Liz. 'Where did the TARDIS console take you?'

'Here!' said the Doctor unexpectedly. 'Same place, same time, different dimensions. A parallel world, Liz. Terrible things happened there. It was this Earth and yet it wasn't. I didn't go back into the past or forwards into the future. I slipped sideways!'

Liz gave him a worried look. 'Doctor, you really ought to rest, you know.'

The Doctor looked at the Brigadier. 'That technician, the one who changed, and went berserk. Has he been caught yet?'

'I'm afraid not, Doctor.'

'What about Stahlman?'

Liz shrugged. 'As difficult as ever.'

'But no worse?' asked the Doctor urgently.

'Not that I've noticed.'

'And how's the drilling progressing?'

Before anyone could answer him, there came a tapping on the hut door.

Liz opened it and a somewhat battered figure marched in. There were minor cuts and bruises on his face, his clothes

113

were torn and dusty and one arm was in a sling – but it was undoubtedly Sir Keith Gold.

The Doctor seemed overjoyed to see him. 'Sir Keith!'

Sir Keith beamed at him. 'My dear fellow, you've come back to us after all.'

'You're not dead!' said the Doctor delightedly.

'No. Though I came very close to it.'

'What happened?' asked the Brigadier.

'Car crash.'

'But you're not dead!' repeated the Doctor.

'You can see he's not dead, Doctor,' said the Brigadier soothingly. He glanced apologetically at Sir Keith. 'The Doctor's been ill, sir.'

'Not dead!' said the Doctor again. 'That's excellent!'

'Yes, I think so too,' agreed Sir Keith politely. He turned to the Brigadier. 'I'm afraid I must lay some very serious charges against Professor Stahlman.'

'You mean he caused your car crash?'

'Well, indirectly. By a mixture of threats and bribery he persuaded my chauffeur to delay my return. The wretched fellow took me miles out of my way. The car crash itself was a genuine accident – the poor devil of a chauffeur was hurt quite badly. I was unconscious for several hours myself.'

The Brigadier nodded. 'And you weren't anywhere near the route from London – which is why I couldn't find you.'

The Doctor was sitting bolt upright by now, looking excitedly from one to the other. 'Don't you see what this means? Not everything runs parallel!'

Sir Keith looked at the Brigadier. 'You did say he'd been ill?'

The Brigadier nodded. 'In a coma, poor chap,' he whispered confidentially.

The Doctor was very much awake now, and in a state of great excitement. 'Yes, of course, of course! It has to be like that. An infinity of universes, an infinite number of choices. That's why free will is not an illusion after all. The pattern can be changed!'

The Brigadier moved unobtrusively over to the wall telephone. 'Hello? Get me the medical section please.'

The Doctor sprang to his feet, snatched the phone from

the Brigadier, and slammed it back on its rest. 'Just you wait a minute. I am not in need of a doctor and I'm not a raving idiot!'

The Brigadier backed away. 'No, no, of course not,' he said soothingly. 'Perhaps you just had a sort of nightmare?'

'He did disappear, you know,' said Liz. 'We saw it.'

The Doctor seized Sir Keith's arm in a painful grip. 'Sir Keith, unless we act now, there's going to be the most terrible disaster imaginable.'

'How can you be so sure, Doctor?'

'Because I've seen it happen!'

The Doctor ran from the hut, and they all hurried after him.

The Doctor could move with amazing speed when he wanted to and by the time the others caught up with him he was confronting an astonished and angry Professor Stahlman in the middle of central control. 'Professor Stahlman! You must stop this drilling immediately!'

'Who let this maniac back in here?' demanded Stahlman.

'I tell you you've got to close down this whole operation – now!'

'Brigadier! You will arrest this man immediately!'

The Doctor raised his voice, addressing the astonished technicians. 'Listen to me, all of you! You must not attempt to penetrate the Earth's crust.'

Stahlman was almost hysterical with rage. 'Brigadier, you heard what I said. Arrest him!'

The Brigadier tried to take the Doctor aside. 'Doctor, please . . .'

But the Doctor's mind was filled with seas of glowing lava, with the terrible spectacle of a world destroyed. He flung the Brigadier aside. 'Get out of my way!' Looking round wildly, the Doctor spotted a massive pipe-wrench projecting from a rigger's tool-bag by the wall. Before anyone could stop him, he ran over to the bag, snatched up the wrench, and began smashing up the nearest console.

'Stop this drilling!' he shouted as he hammered away. 'You don't understand! You've got to stop this drilling!'

'Benton, get some help,' snapped the Brigadier. 'Quickly,

man!' Cautiously he approached the Doctor. 'Doctor, for heaven's sake calm down!'

Stahlman looked on with an air almost of satisfaction. 'You see? Completely demented!'

Benton ran back into the control centre with a couple of UNIT soldiers. Seconds later, the Doctor disappeared under a pile of bodies.

When he was more or less immobilised, the Brigadier reached out and snatched the wrench from the Doctor's hand. 'Get him to the sick-bay. And be careful. I don't want him hurt.'

Struggling furiously, the Doctor was half-dragged half-carried out, a UNIT soldier gripping each arm.

As Liz Shaw looked on with a sort of embarrassed pity, she became aware that the Doctor was calling to her. 'Liz, the computer,' he shouted. 'Missing microcircuit – Stahlman . . . *repair the computer*.' Still struggling and shouting, the Doctor was carried away.

Stahlman was taking full advantage of the situation. 'Brigadier, I hold you responsible for this!'

'You might at least have listened to him,' said Liz firmly. She edged away, moving towards the computer.

Sir Keith stepped forward. 'I should like to speak to you, Professor.'

Stahlman looked disparagingly at him. 'I thought you were supposed to be in London? Been in an accident?'

'That is correct – an accident that was an indirect result of your orders to my chauffeur. You told him to delay my return from London.'

'A ridiculous accusation.'

Sir Keith decided to defer that particular matter until later. 'The Minister requests that you report to him immediately, Professor Stahlman.'

'Does he indeed?'

'There is to be an enquiry into the safety of this project and, if I may say so, into your own conduct.'

'You may hold all the enquiries you please, Sir Keith, after we have penetrated the Earth's crust!' Stahlman turned and marched through the drill-head tunnel.

Petra followed, and found him staring absorbedly at the

drill-shaft. 'The Doctor did only minor damage, Professor. It's being repaired now – it won't cause any delay.'

Stahlman didn't reply.

A little uneasily, Petra went on. 'We shall be switching to the robot cycle in forty-nine minutes.'

'Thank you,' he muttered.

'Is anything wrong, Professor?'

Stahlman swung round to face her. 'It's so cold in here, Petra.'

She looked at him in amazement. 'Cold?' The heat in the drill-head area was almost unbearable.

'Yes. Have the maintenance people raise the temperature.'

'But Professor . . .'

'Do as I ask!' screamed Stahlman.

Petra backed away, and went back through the tunnel.

When she was gone, Stahlman put his hands over his ears to block out the intolerable screeching sound. But it sounded just as loudly inside his head. He moved closer to the drill-shaft. Suddenly Stahlman swung round, calling out to the handful of technicians working in the drill-head area. 'You will leave this area immediately – all of you. I shall handle the final phase of this operation alone. You will stand by in central control'.

The technicians turned from their work, staring disbelievingly at him.

'Get out of here – all of you!' shrieked Stahlman. 'Go on, do as you're told. Get out!'

The terrified technicians began hurrying through the tunnel.

Petra and Greg Sutton watched them file through into central control.

'He's ordered them all out,' said Sutton in disbelief. 'Now do you believe he's cracking up?'

They heard a metallic grinding sound coming from the tunnel.

'The heat-shield,' said Petra. 'He's closing the heat-shield!'

Once outside the control centre the Doctor had calmed down. Now he was walking meekly towards the medical block between two UNIT sentries. He was deep in thought, and he was very worried indeed. Haunted by that nightmarish vision of an exploding Earth, he had acted so violently that his credibility was destroyed. Who would listen to his arguments now? Still, what was done was done. He still had to try everything and anything he could to prevent the coming catastrophe.

The Doctor came to a sudden halt and looked regretfully at the two UNIT soldiers. 'I'm sorry about this gentlemen – I really am!' The Doctor's arms shot out like pistons, out-thrust fingers jabbing the two soldiers beneath their collarbones. They dropped to the ground, and the Doctor turned and ran. He had administered only the lightest of blows and the sentries would soon recover. Minutes later they were struggling to their feet, searching frantically for the Doctor.

Behind him the Doctor heard an alarm-whistle. There were shouts and the sound of running feet as more soldiers were summoned to join in the hunt. By now the Doctor had reached one of the coolant towers. There was a ladder running up one side. With a strange feeling of familiarity, the Doctor began shinning up it. Only when he reached the catwalk that led to the next tower did he realise why.

Shuffling along the catwalk towards him was a grotesque figure in the tattered remnants of a technician's white coveralls. The sleeves had been ripped away, revealing muscular arms covered with coarse black hair ending in huge clawed hands. Roaring and screeching, the creature shuffled towards him.

Apprehensively the Doctor looked around. Hadn't there been two of them last time this had happened – in that other world? But here at least, there was only one. And there was, thank heavens, still a fire-extinguisher attached to the rail. The Doctor grabbed it and blasted the approaching mutant with the cold CO_2 gas. It really was unfair, thought the Doctor, having to overcome the same enemies more than once. Leaping over the writhing mutant, he ran along the catwalk to the other tower, and slid down the ladder. He could still hear the whistle-blasts and shouts of the pursuing soldiers. At least this lot weren't likely to shoot him.

The Doctor began to run. Somehow he had to get back to central control in time.

Alone in the sealed-off drill-head area, Stahlman walked slowly towards the shaft. Thick green slime was oozing from the fractured output pipe. Stahlman ripped off his gloves, revealing both hands covered with coarse hair. Moving with almost ritualistic slowness, he scooped up a double handful of the green slime and smeared it over his face.

He began to change . . .

15

The Doctor Takes a Trip

In central control Petra, Greg Sutton and Sir Keith were listening in horror to the strange sounds coming from the speaker connected to the drill-head area. Moans and snarls and growls, terrifying bestial sounds, were intermingled with a hideous screeching.

Petra was shouting into the mike. 'Professor Stahlman, please! What's happening in there?'

The only reply was a fresh outbreak of hideous snarling.

'Can't you raise the heat shield and get him out?' asked Sir Keith.

Sutton shook his head. 'He's locked it on manual – from the inside.'

Inside the drill-head the creature that had once been Stahlman was writhing in ecstacy at the base of the drill-shaft. Helped by the intense heat, the recessive mutation was taking place with incredible speed. The face twisted and sprouted hair, the eyes flared red, the teeth became great yellowing fangs. Rising to its feet, the mutant beast gave a screech of exultant rage.

The countdown had started.

'*Zero minus two minutes fifty seconds*,' boomed the mechanical voice.

'Over here, all of you,' called Liz suddenly.

The computer had come back to life again, and was spewing out rolls of print-out.

'I found out what was wrong with the computer, Sir Keith,' announced Liz. 'A missing microcircuit, just as the Doctor said. I rigged up a replacement – and there you are!'

Sutton looked at the reels of paper. 'Well? What does it say?'

'It advises us to stop the drilling – at once!'

Sutton turned to Sir Keith. 'Why don't you give the order?'

'I can't.'

'I thought you'd convinced your pal the Minister.'

'So I have. But the order to close down must come from the Professor himself. I have no authority to intervene directly in a technical matter.'

Suddenly the Doctor hurried into the control room. Seeing the computer was working he made his way across to it. 'Well done, Liz.' He snatched up a handful of print-out, scanned it and then looked round the little group. 'Where's Stahlman?'

Liz nodded towards the drill-head. 'He's locked himself in there.'

'Good. Then stop this infernal drilling, Sir Keith. Right now.'

Sir Keith stared helplessly at him, torn by indecision.

'Well, what are you waiting for? Close down the drilling and start filling up that shaft!'

'The data from the computer is not conclusive, Doctor. Nor is Professor Stahlman's behaviour, eccentric though it is. We have no *proof* of an emergency situation . . .'

Even as Sir Keith spoke, the heat-shield was beginning to rise. His attention drawn by the noise, Sir Keith turned to look – and saw before him all the proof that anyone could ever need.

Stahlman was coming out of the tunnel – or rather the creature that had once been Stahlman. The recessive mutation was in its final stage, and scarcely any trace of the human remained. It was the face of a wild beast. The mutant stood looking at them for a moment, swinging its head to and fro, screeching with primitive rage.

Instinctively the Brigadier drew his revolver.

The Doctor put a hand on his arm. 'That's no use. Mr Sutton – the fire extinguishers.'

The Doctor and Sutton ran to the walls, snatched up fire-extinguishers and advanced on the ravening beast that had

121

once been Eric Stahlman. Both opened fire at once, drenching the monster with freezing CO_2 gas. Caught between the blasts of the two extinguishers, the creature's end was mercifully swift. For a moment it screeched and roared, then suddenly it fell writhing to the ground.

The Doctor and Sutton poured on the CO_2 gas until the extinguishers were exhausted and the creature lay still, killed by the sudden massive temperature reduction. There was a moment of appalled silence.

The countdown voice boomed out. '*Zero minus one minute and fifty seconds.*'

'Petra, the drill,' shouted the Doctor. 'Close it down – *now*!'

'How? There's no time!'

'Just cut off the power, Petra,' yelled Sutton.

'But the drill will disintegrate!'

'All the better!' said the Doctor. 'Just hurry!'

Petra raised her voice. 'All technical staff. Stand by for emergency shutdown. Report readiness.'

Seconds later the different power-sections began reporting over the loudspeaker.

'Number 1 section standing by.'

'Section 2 standing by.'

'Section 3 standing by.'

Petra raised her voice in command. 'Shutdown by sections *now*!'

Again the voices rang out. 'Section 1 shut down!'

'Section 2 shut down!'

'Section 3 shut down!'

The roar of the drill went on.

'*Zero minus one minute thirty seconds. Final countdown will commence in thirty seconds.*'

'It isn't stopping,' said the Brigadier.

'We've forgotten the buffer controls in the drill-head,' shouted Sir Keith. 'They slow the drill down by stages. It'll keep going for four or five minutes unless we use the servo cut-out!'

'Come on, Mr Sutton!' said the Doctor.

They raced for the tunnel. Inside the drill-head the heat and the noise were almost intolerable, but the Doctor seemed to ignore them.

Sutton led the way to the buffer control console. 'The servo-switch cut-out has been wrecked!'

'Stahlman!' said the Doctor grimly.

'Can you repair it?'

'I can try.'

'*Zero minus one minute zero seconds and counting. Countdown by seconds commences now! Sixty . . . fifty-nine . . .*'

For those left in central control there was nothing to do but wait and listen as the countdown voice droned remorselessly on, counting away, for all they knew, the remaining seconds of their lives.

'*Forty-five. Forty-four. Forty-three. Forty-two. Forty-one. Forty. Thirty-nine. Thirty-*' Suddenly the voice broke off.

A few moments of tense silence. Then:

'*Attention! Attention! Countdown and drilling stopped at minus thirty-five seconds.*'

They were all too exhausted for cheers but there was a subdued babble of relief.

The Doctor and Sutton staggered out of the tunnel, both streaming with sweat.

'Sir Keith,' said the Doctor a little hoarsely, 'I think you'd better give orders for that shaft to be filled in straight away!'

'Indeed I will Doctor. Indeed I will!'

The Doctor moved over to Stahlman's body and stared down at it for a moment. Perhaps they owed him a debt in a way, he thought. Thanks to Stahlman's urgent need to surrender to the ecstacy of the recessive mutation, Earth – this Earth – had been saved.

The Doctor looked at the little group of his friends, laughing and talking on the other side of the control room. Pain showed in his face for a moment, as he thought of their other selves – those who had not survived. For a moment it was like looking at ghosts.

The Brigadier came over to him, noticing, but misinterpreting, his expression. 'It's all over now, Doctor. I'll sent for a stretcher party, get the poor devil out of there.'

The Doctor nodded and walked out of central control.

After all, he thought as he made his way back to his hut, it wasn't everybody who'd actually seen the end of the world.

The Doctor was in better spirit next morning, as he and Liz Shaw worked on the TARDIS console. 'Shine on Martian moons, up in the sky', he carolled cheerfully. 'Shine on . . .'

There was a rapping on the door, Liz opened it, and the Brigadier and Sir Keith Gold came in. Sir Keith was neat and dapper as usual, though his arm was still in a sling.

'Sorry to disturb you, Doctor. Just popped in to say goodbye.'

'You're leaving then?'

'Everyone is,' said the Brigadier with some satisfaction.

Sir Keith nodded. 'Word came through this morning. This project is officially abandoned.'

'I'm not sorry to hear it. Er – what about the nuclear reactor?'

'They start dismantling it tomorrow.'

'Ah,' said the Doctor hopefully. 'So, there's still time for me to use the power just once more, eh?'

'Of course, Doctor, of course. It's the least we can do.'

'That's very kind, Sir Keith. Very kind indeed. By the way, what's happened to Sutton and Miss Williams?'

'Oh they left early this morning. They asked me to say goodbye.'

'Did they leave together?' asked Liz intrigued.

Sir Keith coughed. 'Well, I believe Mr Sutton is driving Miss Williams back to London.'

The Doctor smiled. 'Nothing like a happy ending, eh Liz?'

Sir Keith said his goodbyes, shook hands all round and departed.

The Brigadier stood watching the Doctor and Liz as they returned to work.

The Doctor looked up and said pointedly. 'Goodbye, Brigadier.'

'Quite a bit of mopping up to do yet, Doctor. I shall be here for a while longer.'

The Doctor muttered something that sounded suspiciously like, 'Pity,' and turned to Liz. 'Well, if they're closing down the reactor, we'd better get a move on.'

'Now just a minute, Doctor,' said Liz slowly.

The Brigadier looked disdainfully at the TARDIS console. 'Can't think why you still bother tinkering with that thing, Doctor, after all the trouble it's caused us.'

Stung by the attack on his beloved TARDIS the Doctor said, 'The trouble it's caused us? What trouble did it cause you?'

'If you hadn't disappeared at such a crucial moment, Doctor, this whole business might have been cleared up much sooner.'

Even Liz thought this was a bit unfair. 'He did try to warn everybody, Brigadier – long before he disappeared.'

'Yes,' said the Doctor indignantly. 'And a fat lot of notice you took!'

The Brigadier said accusingly, 'So you went gallivanting off in a fit of pique!'

The Doctor drew himself up. 'There are times, Brigadier, when you remind me very strongly of your other self. I shall leave at once.' He began adjusting the controls.

Liz watched him in amazement. 'Not in the TARDIS console, Doctor?'

The Doctor gave her a look of dignified reproach. 'Naturally. With the work we did today, the TARDIS console is now fully operational.'

The Brigadier sniffed. 'I seem to have heard that before!'

It was the last straw. The Doctor strode to his power transformer and switched on the power. The console began to hum, lights flashed and the centre column began to rise and fall.

Poised at the controls the Doctor turned to Liz. 'Goodbye, Liz, I shall miss you. But I've had just about as much as I can stand of this pompous, self-opinionated idiot here.' With that the Doctor flicked a couple of switches. Doctor and console promptly disappeared, leaving Liz and the Brigadier open-mouthed.

On this occasion, Liz noticed, Bessie stayed where she was.

Liz looked reproachfully at the Brigadier. 'See what you've done!'

'How was I to know he'd go off like that? The man's so infernally touchy!'

'Well, I shall be very interested to see how you get on without him, Brigadier.'

The Brigadier said sharply. 'May I remind you that you are still a serving member of UNIT, Miss Shaw. I don't entirely care for your tone.'

'I don't much care for yours, either. No wonder the Doctor cleared off.'

A very promising row was interrupted by a cough from behind them. They turned and saw the Doctor standing in the doorway. He was looking for once, far from his usual elegant self. There was mud on his face, in his hair and on his smoking-jacket.

'Welcome back, Doctor,' said the Brigadier, sarcastically.

Liz stared at him in astonishment. 'Where did you go?'

'A few seconds forward in time, a few hundred yards due east in space!'

Liz thought for a moment and then chuckled. 'The rubbish tip?'

'The rubbish tip,' agreed the Doctor ruefully.

'Oh dear!'

The Doctor gave the Brigadier his most ingratiating smile. 'Er – Brigadier, my dear feller! I wonder if I could borrow Benton and a few of your stalwart chaps to give me a hand in bringing the TARDIS console back? It's landed in rather an inaccessible position!'

The Brigadier said thoughtfully, 'Pompous, self-opinionated, idiot I believe you said, Doctor?'

'Well – er, yes. Still, we don't want to bear a grudge for a few hasty words, do we? No! Not after all the years that we've worked together!' The Doctor draped an arm around the Brigadier's shoulders and led him from the hut. 'Now, come along my dear feller – put on a smile . . .'

But it was Liz who was smiling as she watched them go. It was nice having the Doctor back.